SEX AND THE WIDOW MILES

NAN REINHARDT

Sex and the Widow Miles

Copyright © 2013 Nan Reinhardt

Published by Fine Wine Romances

ISBN-13: 978-0-9893968-9-9

ISBN-10: 0989396894

Cover art by Chipperish Media

Cover art and logos Copyright © 2013 Chipperish Media

For Lani, thanks for believing in me and showing me how to believe in myself.

CHAPTER 1

T he elevator doors whispered shut behind me and my
shoulders sagged beneath the weight of an overstuffed
canvas carryon, a leather laptop bag, and my purse. Plush carpet,
four handsome mahogany doors, and warm taupe paint made this
floor of the Lake Terrace building as perfectly appointed as the
lobby and the elevator. Starting down the elegant hallway, I
caught sight of a thin, pale woman in the mirror above the table at
the other end. Frankly, she looked like hammered shit.

God, what happened to you?

The woman was me.

Once again, I wondered what the hell I was doing. That same
thought had occurred to me on the plane from Traverse City,
again while I was standing at the baggage claim in O'Hare
International, and in the cab on the way to Carrie and Liam's new
apartment on Lakeshore Drive. Only the fact that I had to pee
kept me from hitting the elevator button and heading right back to
the airport. I kicked my suitcase to orient the wheels so I could
pull it through the rich carpet.

Heaving a sigh, I dug in my purse for the key Carrie had

pressed into my hand when she hugged me at the airport. "This is a good thing, Jules. I promise."

Opening door number 3, I dragged the suitcase into the tiled foyer, blinking in the winter sunlight that streamed through French windows overlooking Lake Michigan. I didn't want to be here.

"This is crazy," I said aloud to no one at all. "I'm outta here. Just as soon as I pee."

Dropping my coat on the suitcase, I set the heavy carryon on the floor. As I laid the laptop and my purse on the chest in the foyer, I noticed a yellow sticky note stuck to the mirror.

YOU'RE STAYING. Carrie's perfect penmanship in purple marker.

I couldn't help smiling. It was scary how well she knew me. I glanced around. Bathroom. I seriously needed a bathroom. Scurrying through the living room, I found it. A touch of the light switch revealed another note on the mirror above the sink. I pulled it down and read it as I took care of business.

IT'S BEEN A YEAR. IF YOU DON'T MOVE ON NOW, YOU NEVER WILL. Again in bright purple ink.

The familiar clutch of panic hit me when I stuck the note back up on the mirror and washed my hands.

I can't do this. I'm not ready.

Yes, it had been a year since Charlie died, but we'd been married for over thirty. I had no idea how to be anyone but Mrs. Dr. Charles Miles.

How do I find my way alone?

I headed down the hall, ready to collect my belongings and call a cab, but I stopped in the archway between the living room and dining room. Another note, this time a pink one, curled up on the shiny surface of the table.

YOU'RE NOT ALONE. YOU HAVE ALL OF US.

We'd been through all the excuses, Carrie and I, rehashing my sessions with the therapist every Tuesday and Thursday over wine or coffee. Clearly, she could quote my fears chapter and verse.

With a shake of my head and a chuckle, I turned toward the French doors, amazed at the sheer size of the place. The apartment was huge, the dining room table easily seated twelve, and the long hallway that led back to the bedrooms was wide enough for Carrie's antique washstand and two rush-bottom chairs. A grand piano took up one corner of the cavernous living room that she'd managed to make cozy with overstuffed chintz sofas flanking the fireplace, pine tables, pottery lamps, and other French country accents.

Lake Michigan vistas filled the wall of glass doors that led out to a snow-covered balcony. The lake reminded me of home and panic washed over me once more. The urge to flee overwhelmed me. I just wanted to go home. Back to Charlie's big house on the shore, where Gray Flannel cologne lingered in the air and I could still feel him close to me. I wrapped my arms around my middle and bent over, taking deep breaths, willing away the feeling of dread.

When I could breathe again, I wandered through the dining room into a gleaming kitchen, all stainless appliances and warm cherry cabinets. Carrie's personal stamp showed here, too, in the speckled, gray granite countertops and the copper-bottomed pots hanging from hooks above the big stove. On the island next to a bowl of fresh fruit sat a blue Chicago Cubs baseball cap with a white daisy sticking out of the mesh and more daisies hanging off the brim. And there was another note. WEAR THIS, it said. IT'LL MAKE YOU FEEL RIDICULOUS AND RIDICULOUS IS HAPPINESS.

My darling Carrie. Was there ever a better friend in the whole world? How the hell did she manage the post-its and the hat all the way from Michigan? Obviously, she'd enlisted a compatriot in preparing my welcome—no doubt Javier, the personable doorman who'd greeted me when I got out of the cab. I plopped the silly hat on my head, pulling my hair through the hole in the back before checking out my reflection in the glass on the microwave. It was an improvement, so I gave myself a dopey grin and moved on down the hall, peering into Liam's office and the kids' bedrooms.

Another note hung on the double doors to the master suite.

YOU MADE IT THIS FAR. CHARLIE WOULD BE PROUD OF YOU.

Swallowing the lump in my throat, I stepped through the entrance. Carrie's touch was evident again in the white-painted wainscoting, buff walls, and white furniture. A crescent window let sunshine stream in over the French doors that opened onto the balcony. Toile fabric covered a pair of wing chairs on either side of a fireplace. The pattern repeated in the cushion on the dressing table bench, the loveseat at the end of the bed—

The bed. Carrie told me to sleep here in her bed, made up with a white duvet and shams. Oh, dear God. I dropped to the edge of the mattress and covered my face with my hands. My heart hurt and the loneliness washed over me as I realized I'd be sleeping all alone in a bed Charlie has never even seen before. My throat closed up as I fought tears, although a few spilled over into my lashes. Crying within half an hour of arriving was not a good omen.

How do I do this?

I can't.

Suddenly I was so exhausted I could barely sit up straight.

Swiping my damp cheeks with my palms, I leaned back to rest my head on the pillow and bumped into something behind me. Reaching back, I pulled out a big teddy bear, fat and squooshy with velvety white fur. How did I miss him? His sweet goofy face had another post-it stuck right in the middle of his forehead.

IT'S TIME YOU SLEPT WITH A NEW MAN. MEET HORACE.

I couldn't help myself, I giggled. Burying my nose in Horace's soft fur, I sniffed back the tears, and thanked God for a best friend like Carrie Reilly. She'd been right by my side since the funeral and she was still with me, prodding me to move on and making me laugh when all I wanted to do was sit down and cry. With one swift kick, I let my shoes drop to the floor and curled up in the center of the bed, my arms full of fuzzy polar bear.

I had no idea how to get rid of the overwhelming sense of loss, and I sighed as I flopped over onto my back and hugged the stuffed bear close. According to the therapist, you move on with your life, and that was what this trip was all about. It was all about getting away, finding a new focus.

So now, here I was, crying into a teddy bear in the middle of Carrie and Liam's bed, and trying to figure out what I was going to do with myself in Chicago for the next few weeks. Dr. Benton was wrong, a change of scenery wasn't going to help. It was the same grief, just a different venue.

I closed my eyes against the burn of threatening tears, and worked on the focusing exercises the therapist had given me when a door closing somewhere in the apartment brought me upright with a start.

Heavy footsteps sounded in the foyer.

Oh, God. Somebody was in here. Did I forget to lock the door? Hell, did I even *close* the door? I couldn't remember. Leaping from the bed, I scanned the room for something to defend myself with, and my eyes lit on a baseball bat leaning against the wall between the bed and the nightstand. Ah, Carrie's trusty bat—her response when Liam suggested buying a handgun after an apartment in the building down the block was burgled.

Great. My first hour in the big city and I'm going to be murdered all over Carrie's beautiful white bed.

Heart pounding, I grabbed the bat and tiptoed over to peer around the door.

"Carrie? Are you in here?" called a deep voice laced with concern.

Okay, so maybe it wasn't a murderer. But it also wasn't Javier, the doorman, whose voice was higher and accented. How dare someone just walk in without knocking and scare the daylights out of me like this? What the hell's wrong with ringing the damn doorbell?

The footsteps were headed down the hallway now, so I used my anger to build courage and stepped out from behind the door. I looked ridiculous in the daisy hat, with a giant polar bear tucked under one arm and brandishing a Louisville Slugger. But who cared? I was *supposed* to be here, this guy certainly wasn't.

He was tall and his spiky blond hair, backlit by the sun, shone in a gold halo around his head. "Do I know you?" he asked. "Are you Jules?"

Irritation battled with relief as I realized the guy, who looked vaguely familiar, was probably harmless. Still, he should've rung the bell, not just walked in.

Jerk.

I was beat and frustrated and so over everyone and everything that I brushed past him and headed for the kitchen.

"I'm the widow fucking Miles," I said. "And I need a drink."

CHAPTER 2

"Easy, Slugger. I didn't mean to scare you." The man trailed behind me into the kitchen.

Slugger?

Oh, the bat. Cute, very cute.

I finally recognized him. He was Liam's business manager Will… something. The guy Carrie had told me lived diagonally across the hall in Apartment 2. I'd actually seen him around Willow Bay when he'd stopped in to meet with Liam, but beyond attending a couple of the same New Year's Eve parties at Reilly's, we'd never really had any interaction.

"Try the wine fridge." He cocked his head toward the wine cooler below the counter next to the sink. "Unless you want something stronger. In that case, liquor's in the cabinet under the island."

I pulled out some Riesling and set the wine, the bear, and the bat on the island before yanking on the first drawer I came to in search of a wine opener.

The guy sat down in a tall wrought iron stool and gazed at me, a small smile playing on his lips.

Two drawers later, I let out a disgusted breath. "Corkscrew?"

"Over there, top drawer." He pointed. "Glasses in the cabinet above the wine cooler."

I scowled. The cabinets were glass-front, for God's sake. I'd figured out where the damn wineglasses were. Even though I was irritated with him for scaring a couple of years off my life, and I wasn't really in the mood for entertaining, I held up a second glass. Since I didn't intend to stay past one quick glass of wine, I figured why not be at least a little gracious.

"Sure, I'd love some wine. Thanks," he said. "I'm Will Brody, by the way. Liam's business manager, neighbor, friend, and all-around good guy." If he hadn't already turned on the overhead lights, his smile would've lit up the kitchen. "And you're Carrie's best friend, Jules, right? They told me to expect you."

Churlish isn't usually my style, but I wasn't in any frame of mind to get drawn into exchanging pleasantries with this guy, particularly since I'd be gone in less than an hour anyway. However, I gave him a grudging nod as I pulled the cork from the bottle. "Yes. Julianne Miles."

"Very nice to meet you."

After I poured, he held his glass up and touched his rim to mine. "To... new beginnings?"

"To finding me a cab to the airport." I downed half the wine in one gulp.

"You're leaving? But you just got here."

"This was a stupid idea. I don't belong here." I swilled the rest of the Riesling and then refilled my glass.

Okay, so maybe I'd stay for two drinks.

"How do you know that? You haven't even given it a chance." Will toyed with the corkscrew, removing the cork from the spiral and then twisting it back on again before nodding his head toward another bar stool. "Have a seat, why don't you?"

His smile disarmed my anger, but only a little. I was fuming and I wasn't even sure anymore who I was mad at. Will Brody, for scaring the crap out of me? Carrie, for making me come here when all I wanted to do was stay in the warm cocoon of my house on the shore? The therapist, for forcing me to rethink… well, everything? Charlie, for fucking dying in the first place?

Yes. Yes to all of those.

My conscience nudged me. *Or maybe you're just mad at yourself.* I ignored it and topped off my beverage before plopping down in the stool across from Will Brody.

"How did you get in here?" The question sounded surlier than I intended, but he just responded with a friendly smile.

"Normally, I use a key. Today, you left the door wide open. I know Carrie and Liam are back in Michigan, so I thought something was wrong. Then I remembered Carrie telling me you'd be here in the late afternoon. This is a very safe building, but I don't recommend leaving the door open."

"I didn't realize I had." I sipped the wine a little slower, letting the crisp fruity taste linger on my tongue. He was studying me, and suddenly I was very aware of my bare feet, my wrinkled blouse, and oh, damn, that goofy hat. I yanked it off my head, but my hair became knotted in the plastic hooks in the back when I pulled. "Shit."

Before I could release it, Will hopped up and came to my aid, gently untangling the long strands and then handing me the cap. "Nice hat." He grinned, white teeth gleaming against his tanned face as he returned to his seat.

"A welcome gift from Carrie." Heat flushed my cheeks, so I changed the subject. "Where'd you get a tan like that in January? Florida?"

"Italy. I've been over in Europe checking out venues for Liam's summer tour."

"That's a sweet gig."

"No complaints."

"Aren't you kinda young to be someone's business manager?"

What had Carrie said about Will? My mind was a blank. Sitting across from me, he looked like my oldest son, Kevin, who was also tall and blond and a very nice man at twenty-nine years old. Will could be a little older, but probably not much.

"I'm thirty-nine." He reached for the wine bottle and refilled both our glasses.

I did the math in my head. Thirteen years between us. He was a baby. "To me, that's young, kid." One more glass of wine and then I was calling a cab and heading back to the airport.

"You're not *that* much older than me." His eyes twinkled and in the light they appeared almost teal blue. Aquamarine. Had to be contacts. Nobody's eyes were naturally that shade of blue.

"I'm fifty-two." I blurted. "Old enough to be your mother."

"Well, only if my mother had been a very young teen mom, which I assure you she wasn't." A long pause set in before he spoke again. "I'm sorry about your husband. Carrie told me about him."

I shrugged and shifted on my stool. "Thanks. Ironic, huh? A heart surgeon dying of a massive heart attack?"

"Life can be ironic. How long has it been?"

"It's been a year… barely."

"You doing okay?"

When I met his steady gaze over the wine glasses, his eyes were warm and full of concern. He wasn't simply making small talk. He was genuinely interested, but I couldn't imagine why. He didn't know me.

"I don't know. I guess. I feel so… empty… so displaced. I don't know where I belong anymore or who I am. I've been Mrs. Dr. Charles Miles since I was nineteen years old." The words just poured out of me like they did with Dr. Benton or with Carrie. Why was I telling him all this stuff? I resisted the urge to clap my hand over my mouth, but with each question he asked, I dumped more details on the table.

"But that's not all you are," he pointed out. "What about your own career? Didn't Carrie tell me you're a model?"

"I *was* a model, but I think that's pretty much over." I gave a short laugh. "We were planning our retirement when he—" I was scared that saying the word would start the tears burning in my eyes. I blinked and focused on my wine, and for a moment, my mind slipped back to what might have been.

Just a few months before he died, Charlie had been due to retire from his job as chief of cardiac surgery at St. Anne's Hospital in Traverse City, and I was going to be done with modeling after the Macy's spring line shoot in October. We'd planned to rent a house in Aruba and spend the first winter of retirement on the beach, drinking ourselves stupid and making love until we ached.

All that was gone now. Charlie was dead, and I'd spent the last year trying to figure out a way to go on without him. But I hadn't been able to get motivated to do anything at all. The therapist had helped... and so had Carrie, although I still wasn't convinced this trip was necessary.

When I glanced up, Will was watching me, concern furrowing his brow.

"It's been a... rough road," I finally said.

"Did you try one of those grief support groups? My grandma went to one when Pops passed. Seemed to help her."

"I went to one at the library in Willow Bay after I started with the therapist. Carrie made me go." I exhaled a bitter laugh. "Lord, it was depressing. Some of those women had been there for years. I could tell they'd been rehashing their dead husbands' lives for ages... meeting after meeting." I smoothed my hair back off my face. "No way that was gonna work. But the therapist started me on an antidepressant and—" I broke off with a self-conscious shrug.

What the hell was the matter with me? Spilling my guts to a

perfect stranger? Even if he was a close friend of Carrie and Liam, I shouldn't be sharing intimate details of my life with him. I sounded as pitiful as those women in the grief group. God, I didn't want to be that tragic figure. Not anymore.

"And what?" Will gave me an encouraging smile.

Was this guy for real? Why on earth was he interested in hearing an old widow's tale?

I closed my eyes. My tension eased as the wine worked its magic. I was going to have to find some food pretty soon or I would pass out on the kitchen floor. Surely Carrie had something to munch on in this vast kitchen.

Almost as if he'd read my mind, Will said, "You could probably use something to eat. Why don't I order us a pizza?"

"That's okay. I'll just find some crackers before I call a cab."

"Oh come on, you need more than crackers, and I'm hungry too. Guido's down the block makes a great hand-tossed and they deliver. I'll order and then I'll haul your trunk over here. It's sitting in my living room. It arrived this morning and since Carrie had it expressed to me, Javier just had them put it at my place."

"Oh, good God, she sent all those clothes here? I told her to just give them to a charity up there." I rolled my eyes and rose to ransack the cupboards for something crunchy and salty. My first step wobbled. I clutched the granite counter to keep from falling on my ass.

Will was next to me in a heartbeat, his hand on my elbow, helping me back to the stool.

"Better get us both some food *now*. Wine on an empty stomach ain't workin'." He pulled his phone out and in a few short taps ordered a pizza online. "It'll be here in about twenty-five minutes. Carrie's gotta have something around here we can fill in with." He went right to the pantry off the kitchen and came back with a bag of pretzels, a box of crackers, and a can of peanuts. A trip to the huge Subzero fridge produced two kinds of cheese, a couple of varieties of dip, and two bottles of water.

Reaching under the bar, he pulled out small paper plates and cocktail napkins that made me smile. They were imprinted with, WINE—IT'S HOW CLASSY PEOPLE GET TRASHED. It was pure Carrie Reilly. Will grinned, too, as he pulled lids off the dip and opened packages of cheese.

"Dig in." He offered me the bag of pretzels.

What was the use of fighting it at this stage? Obviously, I wasn't going anywhere in the next couple of hours. I was tired, hungry, and more than a little buzzed. The thought of a cab ride was bad enough, but another few hours at O'Hare? That simply was not going to happen tonight.

Okay, Carrie, you win this one.

The notes, the bear, the cozy apartment, and a kind, handsome neighbor could be construed as unfair tactics, but you win. I'm here. I'm staying.

At least tonight.

CHAPTER 3

T he pizza tasted incredible. I devoured two huge pieces, washing it down with the water. Carrie would've been delighted to see my appetite returning. She'd been enticing me with casseroles, huge fresh salads, and endless baked goods for months. When Will offered to open a bottle of Chianti he had at his place, I declined, even though it was tempting to simply drink until sleep overcame me. Dr. Benton would've frowned on mixing that much wine with the antidepressants, and besides, I had some thinking to do. Even though I'd resigned myself to staying the night, I still wasn't sure I was going to unpack and settle in for the winter.

While we ate, Will told me a little about the places he'd been, arranging dates and venues for Liam's summer tour in Europe. It was clear Will loved his job managing Liam's career as a symphony conductor, and hearing about the different cities where Liam would be guest conducting orchestras gave me a sneak peek into Carrie's summer. It was going to be wondrous—Athens, London, Munich, Paris, Rome, even Budapest.

Charlie and I had talked about doing Europe when he retired. I wanted to backpack, take the trains, and stay at tiny inns, but

Charlie longed for luxury hotels, five-star restaurants, and a hired car and a driver. It didn't matter anymore. We wouldn't be touring Europe together.

Before he left, Will helped me clean up, which entailed tossing the paper plates and bottles in the recycle bin, rinsing out wine glasses, and closing up the pizza box so he could take it home. He even earned my grudging respect for not trying to manhandle my huge trunk all by himself. Instead he welcomed my assistance in bringing it across the hall. I couldn't deny I felt better, so as he left, I thanked him more graciously than I'd greeted him earlier.

I had to grin as I locked the door behind him and heard him call, "The chain too, Jules."

I latched the chain. Apparently, he was taking Carrie's instructions to "keep an eye on Jules for me" to heart. I appreciated how he'd made the whole evening so easy with his relaxed manner and no probing questions about what I planned to do with my life. It was nice to simply listen to his travel stories and get out of my own head for an hour or so.

Switching off lights as I made my way back to the bedroom, I suddenly realized that I was probably tired enough to fall asleep without any help from the little pink pills. A shower sounded lovely, so as soon as I hit the bedroom door, I dug in my suitcase for my toothbrush, face wash, and soap. The canvas tote on the floor caught my eye and I remembered my cell phone was still turned off from the flight.

Whoops.

I powered it on and saw that I had five missed calls, three of which were from my oldest son, Kevin. I'd no more seen the list of missed calls than my phone rang, vibrating against my palm. *Kevin.* I answered it and tried to put some life into my voice. "Hey, honey."

"Mom, thank God! I've been trying to get a hold of you all day."

"I was flying today, remember? I'm at Aunt Carrie's house in Chicago." Unbuttoning my blouse, I sat on the edge of the bed.

"Well, where was your cell phone?" Kevin's deep voice reminded me so much of Charlie's, a pang pierced my heart.

"I just turned it back on. Sorry, I forgot to do it when I landed."

"You need to keep it charged and on your person," Kevin explained as though he were talking to a child. I guess dealing with me was great practice for becoming a father. "First of all, we all feel safer if you have it near. And second, I want to be able to get you if Meg goes into labor."

"She's not in labor, is she?" My heart speeded up. My first grandchild wasn't due for another couple of months. "It's way too soon."

"No, she's fine, she's at work. I was just making a point."

"Oh, okay. I'll keep it close, I promise."

"So, how was the flight?" he asked. "Was it tough? Are you okay?"

"I'm okay. But it's been a long day." My jaw ached with the effort of holding back a yawn, so I gave up. All I wanted to do was shower and go to sleep. "Honey, thanks for checking on me. I'm going to turn in now, I'm just exhausted."

"Mom, wait, please." The concern in his voice traveled loud and clear across the miles between us. "Why don't you come out here and be with us instead of spending the winter in Chicago? It's warmer. We've got the sleeper sofa now. You can help us decorate the nursery."

"I'll come out when Meg has the baby, I promise." I felt terrible letting him down, but it had taken all I had in me to make *this* trip. And I still hadn't decided to stay. Putting on a happy face each day for my son and his family was more than I could do.

"Mom… "Kevin hesitated. "We love you so much. We're worried about you." His sweet tone brought tears to my eyes.

I couldn't stand the thought of blubbering on the phone to the poor kid again, so I swallowed hard. "I know you do, baby. I love you too." I put my hand over the receiver for a moment as a tear trickled down my face. "I'm good, l really am. I'll call you in the morning and text you some pictures of this apartment, okay? It's pretty incredible."

We talked another minute or two. I convinced him all was well. They were so worried. The kids, Carrie, Liam, Eliot, Margie, and Noah. And even Will's expression as he sat across from me eating pizza had the same concern. Everyone in my life was watching and waiting for me to reassure them that I'd be fine. For the first time in a year, that seemed like it might be possible, but for tonight, I just needed a shower and a bed.

Stripping off my clothes, I stopped as I passed the bathroom vanity mirror. Carrie was right; I *did* look like hammered shit. My cheeks were hollow. Shadows smudged purple under my eyes. My hair looked good though because I'd had it cut and high-lighted right before I left. But when I leaned into the mirror, I saw silver strands among the darker blonde. And even though I had picked up a few pounds over the holidays, I was getting flabby. My breasts were starting to sag, the flesh of my arms wasn't as firm, and my hip bones showed.

Charlie would be appalled. He was always so proud of my toned body and thick, shiny hair.

"You're the ultimate arm candy, Jules." I could hear his warm voice in my head.

Not any more, my love.

I straightened my shoulders as I clipped my hair up off my neck.

I knew I had to use this time in Chicago to figure myself out —to get a grip. When I sat in Dr. Benton's office, it all sounded so very reasonable. Grieving was a process. I was stuck in that process. I understood that, but until now, I didn't *want* to get a grip. Charlie's death was still too raw, and my sorrow filled me up and wore me out. The antidepressants had helped—before I started them, driving to the grocery had been impossible, let alone flying to a new city. But even though the airports and cabs today had left me drained, for the first time in over a year, I was intrigued to see what tomorrow would bring.

Anger welled up inside me as I twisted sideways and eyed my nude body in profile. I'd spent all those months lying in bed, sucking down coffee and wine, missing Charlie so much I couldn't even think straight. But it didn't bring him back. Months of therapy had shown me one important thing—it *was* time for a change.

Turning away from the ghost in the mirror, I wrenched on the water and stepped into the cold shower. I screeched as it hit my body, but I needed that splash of icy water to remind me I was still alive. The water warmed up and I stood under the stream, allowing my tensions to drain away with the suds from the soap. It felt delicious and comfortable and… right.

In that moment, I made up my mind to stay in Chicago for the winter. Carrie and Liam's building had a gym and a pool. I could work out, get my strength and muscle tone back. Carrie probably knew of a decent spa so I could have a facial and a body wrap. I'd call her tomorrow, or perhaps I'd bundle up and take a walk, try to find my way around the neighborhood. Maybe even go by the agency and see some of my old friends from the catalogue shoots. Sharon and Deb and Maureen had all been in the Macy's spring and Christmas ads, looking as glamorous as ever. It would be fun to do lunch and catch up on their lives.

The bedside lamps cast a soft glow in the room as I pulled on my nightgown and got my Kindle and iPod from my carryon. Tossing back the covers, I plumped the pillows and slipped into the warm flannel sheets. Carrie hated flannel sheets. She'd put them on her bed especially for me. My lips curved up in a smile at how hard she'd worked to make the perfect welcome for me, and a twinge of guilt tweaked the back of my mind for being surly to her neighbor earlier.

Plugging the buds into my ears, I switched on the music. It was actually Charlie's iPod. Mine was at home somewhere, maybe on the desk in the kitchen buried under a pile of magazines. The first thing on his playlist was Norah Jones, and I smiled as her sultry voice filled my head. We danced to "Shoot the Moon" when we were on Mackinac Island for our anniversary —it was the last time we'd danced together.

The memory was sweet, but not pulling me down into the abyss of despair that so many other memories had in the last months. That surprised me. Maybe I *was* getting better. Carrie had been so scared for me, worried that I might do something stupid, maybe try to join him. To be honest, the thought had crossed my mind one day not long after the funeral. But I'd shoved it away almost as soon as it had entered my head and instead, let sleep and wine dull the pain.

But after I'd started seeing Dr. Benton, when I finally found the courage to pack and make this trip, it was the beginning of acknowledging that Charlie wasn't coming home ever again. I'd even agreed to let Carrie and Liam clean out his belongings from the bedroom closet and paint while I was in Chicago.

My thoughts turned to Will Brody, who had made the transition into my new life in Chicago just a bit easier tonight. Maybe it was all going to be okay. This trip might be a turning point.

Almost palpably, my grief had begun to subside.

CHAPTER 4

I hauled the suitcase onto the bed and with a grunt, unzipped it. Why in God's sweet name had Carrie packed all these skirts, jackets, dresses, and shoes? Where the hell did she think I was going? It looked like she'd packed my entire wardrobe, but I knew my closet in Willow Bay was still half full. I had entirely too many clothes, although you'd never know it from my current appearance. Glancing down, I frowned at my yoga pants, white tank top, and comfortable old MSU hoodie.

When I'd arrived a few days earlier, I opened the trunk and unpacked several pairs of jeans and pants, hung up a few soft shirts, sweaters, and skirts. I pulled out a couple of pairs of comfy yoga pants, all my underwear and socks, and my swimsuit and put them in the drawers Carrie had emptied for me in her antique dresser. I'd found my favorite jogging shoes and my boots, plus a couple of other pairs of shoes that I loved. Now I had to figure out what to do with all the rest of the stuff she'd packed.

Things were going along pretty well so far. The apartment was huge, light, and airy and yet cozy, warm, and comfortable. Exactly what someone would expect Carrie's home to be. Her spirit surrounded me here and made the transition from my house on the shore to this citified atmosphere surprisingly easy. The longing for Charlie's house—for Charlie—was abating somewhat. Oh, I still thought about him several times each day, but I was focusing on getting to know Chicago and the neighborhood.

I'd made friends with Javier, the doorman—a charming fellow with a Frito Bandito moustache and fourteen grandchildren. He'd given me a grand tour that included the workout room and a wonderful lap pool in the basement of the building. I'd already swum an hour's worth of laps twice, and my shoulders were screaming at me, but it felt so good to be active and moving my body again. If I kept up the physical exercise, I was sure I'd be able to cut back on the antidepressants. I'd found a great coffee shop that served an excellent white chocolate mocha just down the street from the apartment. I'd even made an appointment with the new therapist, Dr. Jardin. All in all, I was settling in. Carrie would be proud.

Will Brody had been friendly and helpful, checking in on me several times, giving me directions to the dry cleaners, the drugstore, and a little grocery on the corner that had incredible produce even though it was a typical bitter Midwest winter. I couldn't help wondering what he did all day. Did he have an office or did he work from his apartment? We'd met in the pool once or twice when I gone down to swim even though I picked mid-morning to avoid the early birds. I tried to imagine what a symphony conductor's manager's job would involve, but all I came up with was what I already knew. He traveled to check out orchestras and venues, set up Liam's schedule of appearances, and managed his finances.

Maybe I could talk to Will about my finances. Carrie told me he used to be a stockbroker when I'd asked her about him earlier in the week. Charlie always took care of our money and according our attorney back home, I was okay. Charlie had left me well taken care of with life insurance and the investments he'd made.

I'd always managed my own money from the modeling and my savings account was comfortable, but I was certain that the money could be working harder, plus the stock market had always fascinated me. I had some spare cash to play with, and Will might be just the person to give me some investing advice.

Later I planned to set up Charlie's laptop on the table in the breakfast nook and try to figure out the wireless Internet connection. I'd brought his because it was newer, and I could put my hands on it quicker as I packed. I figured I could always call Liam or Will if I couldn't get it to work, but Javier told me to use the building password and I'd be online in no time. I wanted to email the kids and give them my address here. My daughter, Renee, was in Africa with a group of nurses, and email was about the only way to communicate with her. Her twin, Ryan, was down at IU med school in Indianapolis. He had a crazy schedule, so texting was how he communicated. Kevin told me he'd sent me some pictures of Meg's ever-expanding belly.

Yeah, I needed to get online.

Late afternoon sun streamed into the window making the apartment warm and snug even though it was only twenty-two degrees outside. I sorted clothes into stacks and then put them in boxes I'd grabbed from the shipping store down the street. Perhaps there was a charity or consignment shop nearby I could take them to. They were all gorgeous designer labels, most of them from catalog shoots—a little bonus for modeling the outfits. Plus Charlie had shopped like a damned fashion expert. He loved dressing me. Teased me constantly about learning my fashion sense from him. That probably should have offended my feminist sensibilities, but he did it with such charm, it was impossible to get mad. I didn't need all these clothes now. Perhaps someone else could get some real use out of them. I made a mental note to call Carrie and find out where she took her things.

I was so focused on sorting through dresses, blouses, skirts, and jackets that the sound of music startled me when it chimed through the roomy apartment. Trust Liam to have a doorbell that played Bach. I hummed along with "Jesu, Joy of Man's Desiring" as I peeked through the peephole to see Will Brody in the hallway, tall and brawny, his blond hair slightly mussed.

"Hey, Slugger," he greeted me as I opened the door. Okay, so he was a nicknamer, but I didn't mind. It was kind of cute.

I couldn't decide if the careless hairstyle was deliberate or if he'd just gotten up from a nap, but I resisted the urge to put my fingers in that thick mop and feel for styling products. Loafing against the open doorjamb, he was tall, so tall that I had to tip my head back to look up into his eyes. And they were great eyes. Blue, like the Caribbean Sea, and friendly as he grinned that killer grin. God almighty, this guy *was* handsome.

Blinking, I realized I was staring and hadn't even said hello yet. "Come on in, Will." I opened the door wider to let him inside.

"How's it going? Hope it doesn't seem like I'm hovering, but it's gonna snow tonight and I was headed to the market. I thought I'd see if you needed anything." He sauntered in, thumbs tucked in the pockets of his jeans. I couldn't help observing how great those jeans hugged his body and the fact that I noticed shocked the hell out of me.

I followed him into the living room. His shoulders were broad in the navy sweater he wore—he had the California surfer look going big time in spite of living in Chicago. Why the hell was I noticing that? And why had my heart suddenly speeded up? This was the same guy I'd snarled at a few days ago. Nothing had changed.

"I'm okay, thanks." My voice sounded strained. "Carrie packed my entire wardrobe, so I'm sorting through it."

"We're due about six inches. You set for food?" He turned those gorgeous eyes on me and my belly flipped.

What the hell? Was this some kind of reaction from the meds, or was I missing Charlie and sex so much that my imagination was running completely amuck? Sex had been such a non-issue since Charlie died, I hadn't even had the desire to try the vibrator Carrie had given me for my birthday last summer. Yet here I was, belly reeling like I was on rollercoaster just because Will offered me a sweet smile. Is this what happened when depression started easing?

Oh, no! Helluva time for my libido to make a reappearance.

His brow furrowed slightly. "Do you want to come with me? We should hit the market before it gets too—" He caught my eye.

I leaned against the sofa, arms crossed under my breasts, simply gazing at him. I was frozen there, unable to respond, my mouth as dry as a desert. Was I actually lusting after a guy who's practically a stranger? And almost young enough to be my son?

Yep. Desire curled in my lower belly, although it had been such a long time, I barely recognized the sensation. Blood rushed to my cheeks and my body warmed as I stared at him standing there in Liam and Carrie's living room, looking like an MTV beach party host.

Will's face changed from friendly curiosity to something else, something indefinable. But when his gaze locked on mine, his expression altered completely. Concern and worry creased his brow as lust literally took my breath away. A major menopausal heart palpitation began coming on. My pulse pounded in my throat and in my ears as he walked toward me. I pressed my fist to my chest.

"Hey, are you all right?" Reaching for me, he leaned down to peer into my face. He was so close his cinnamon-sweet breath warmed my cheek. With a little sympathetic cluck, he tugged me into his arms. "Julie, it's okay... it's okay. I know this must be hard."

He'd completely misread me, but my arms slid around his waist anyway. I pressed myself against his chest, inhaling the scent of him—clean, crisp, woodsy. Dear God, I'd forgotten how it good it felt to be in a strong man's arms. How delicious to have a man's hands smoothing over my back, a man's body warm and hard next to mine. He stroked my hair, murmuring little comforts. Shamelessly, I basked in his embrace.

Will's hand came up between us, the back brushing my breast as he tucked one finger under my chin to lift my face to his, and the atmosphere between us heated up immediately. Our eyes held as those aqua lights darkened. His lips hovered over mine for a few seconds before, with a groan, he kissed me. He certainly wasn't misreading me now. It was a great kiss—a little tentative at first, but when I didn't protest, he increased the pressure. His tongue stroked into my mouth as my pulse kicked into overdrive.

Tunneling his fingers into my hair, his hand cupped the back of my head, holding me still for his fervent kiss. I couldn't help responding, meeting his tongue with my own as a fire stoked between my legs. My nipples pebbled with the touch of his chest next to mine. My hands crept up his back, tracing the muscles there as my tongue sought his.

The therapist had warned me the meds I was taking might dampen my sex drive. Apparently, she hadn't counted on Will Brody, because my libido was on point. I slipped one hand under his sweater only to find his undershirt keeping me from the warmth of his bare skin.

When he slid his other hand down my back to my behind, pressing my lower body to his, evidence of his arousal was unmistakable. The feel of his erection against my belly splashed icy reality over me. Oh, sweet Christ in heaven! The last time a hard-on pushed into my stomach like that was on Mackinac Island.

Charlie!

What the hell was I thinking? I couldn't do this… no way. Not with Charlie lingering in my mind and heart.

Wrenching myself from his lips and arms and gasping for breath, I backed a few feet away and bumped into the grand piano next to the huge window that overlooked Lake Michigan. My elbow hit a framed picture, which sent a couple more clattering over and one skittering across the floor.

I wrapped my arms around my waist as my words came out on a little choked sob. "Oh, God... I... I... "

"Julie?" He blinked, confusion and lust evident on his face as guilt washed over me.

"I'm sorry, Will." I could still feel his heat on my body and his lips on my mouth—the feeling only increased my shame. "I'm sorry. I'm so sorry."

"I'm not. Not one bit." It was the last thing on Earth I expected him to say.

"*What?*"

"Look, I'm attracted to you." His hand shook as he ran it over his mouth and then he dropped down onto the arm of the sofa as if his legs wouldn't support him. "I can't help it. You got me with the Louisville Slugger and that dopey hat. Why do you think I've been hanging around so much for the past few days?"

"Good Lord, Will, you hardly know me. Plus, I'm old enough to be your mother." I blurted it out without thinking.

"You are not." He scowled at me.

"You're closer to my son's age than you are to mine. I'm way too old for you."

I wasn't even sure why we were having this discussion. Getting involved with Will Brody—hell, getting involved with *any* man—was out of the question. I belonged to Charlie Miles, I always would. Will would be nothing more than a way to scratch an itch. An itch I'd mistakenly believed had died with my husband. I couldn't do that to such a nice guy. Besides in my current state of menopausal moodiness, no way could I handle playing cougar to Will's teenaged crush.

"Bullshit." Will's voice trembled. "I'm thirty-nine years old—in most cultures that's considered an adult."

"Well, I'm fifty-two and in *this* culture that's considered practically a senior citizen." My heart still pounded. My face was feverish and a trickle of sweat ran between my breasts.

Oh great, a hot flash.

I was mortified and frustrated… and longing to hurl myself back into his arms and kiss him stupid. I let my eyes slide away from his as I zipped my hoodie up to my neck. Swallowing hard, I turned to stare out at Lake Michigan glistening in the sunset nine stories below. How could I have let this happen? What was wrong with me? Was I *that* starved for affection? For sex?

God, how humiliating.

As unobtrusively as I could, I rubbed my tank top between my breasts to try to dry off and blew a frustrated breath into my bangs in an effort to gain some composure.

Dammit, dammit.

It wasn't that I couldn't handle a guy making a pass. Photographers and male models—the ones that were straight anyway—made passes all the time. It was how they entertained themselves during a long shoot. But this was *Will,* Liam's best friend, and I could tell from his face that the kiss wasn't simply a pass. It was a declaration. When I turned back around, he was slumped on the arm of the leather sofa, staring at me. The look in his eyes was unfathomable and I was at a complete loss as to what to say to him.

Suddenly he stood up, equilibrium seemingly restored. "I'm ordering us take-out," he said, apropos of nothing. "How about Thai? Do you like peanut chicken? We can have it at my place because I have beer and I'm sure you don't. So come on, we'll go over and watch an old movie. Carrie told me you love Katherine Hepburn. I have *The African Queen* on Blu-ray."

"Will—"

He held up his hand to stop me. "We're not done, Jules—not by a long shot. I don't believe for one minute that kissing you was a mistake, but we'll let it be for now." He grinned and my heart speeded up all over again. "Relax, okay? Obviously, you're not ready, so I'm not going to push you. I promise. Dinner, beer, and a movie—two friends—nothing more."

He started for the door and slowly, I followed him, still blushing and confused. My mind was whirling. Frankly, I wasn't worried about *him*, I was worried about *me*. Will had touched a place in me I thought was dead. Finding out that it wasn't shocked me right down to my socks. My body was a morass of lust and longing, and this sweet guy was the one who'd awakened it in me. Dear God, how was I going to close this Pandora's Box? I had to. No question about that. But even as I tamped down the feelings, I watched him, big and blond and broad, and heat seared in me.

"I have to tell you about what I saw in Paris." He opened the door and held it for me. His tone was completely conversational, the flush gone from his cheeks.

How in the world did he switch gears so easily? When I passed by him, the sexy male scent of him nearly did me in, and in my head, I cursed the whole concept of pheromones. I stole a quick peek at his face. Not so much Mr. Cool as he seemed. His eyes betrayed him—they were still dark with emotion.

He shoved one hand his pocket as I slipped past him, and his voice quavered ever so slightly as he continued, "There was this guy on the Metro with a monkey…"

CHAPTER 5

A couple of days later, I loaded the boxes and garment bags of clothes into Carrie's Prius and headed for the charity she'd told me about on the phone the night before. Will's Google maps indicated the place was only a few miles from Carrie and Liam's Lakeshore Drive apartment building. She was thrilled I was donating the clothes, and I wondered if secretly she'd hoped I'd do just that when she over-packed me so vigorously, knowing I would never need all those suits and dresses. The charity she'd recommended—a place called *La Belle Femme*—was part of a shelter that served battered women in Chicago.

"It's a wonderful place, Jules," she'd told me last night on the phone.

I could almost see Carrie curling up in the big armchair in her family room as she settled in for a long chat. The mental picture caused a twinge of homesickness for my big house next door to hers on the shore as she waxed enthusiastic about the shelter and the shop.

"The Chicago Symphony does a benefit for them every fall, and Sarah Everett—the woman who runs the shop—is a gem. She used to be an Atlanta socialite and lived in the lap of luxury, but her husband abused her terribly. When she escaped him a couple ofyears ago, she devoted her life to helping other battered and abused women. She came to the shelter for protection, but stayed on. Her settlement from her divorce helped them open up the boutique."

"These clothes aren't geared for that type of place," I'd protested. "All these designer suits and dresses. How can *they* use them?"

"Actually, your stuff's perfect! This little boutique gives their clothes away—they help women get back on their feet and prepare them to go out on job interviews. So many of these women have been mentally and emotionally bruised, as well as physically. Honestly, they don't have the confidence to pick out a pot roast, let alone dress themselves for a job interview. Sarah and her staff are terrific." Carrie's enthusiasm was contagious. I was getting curious and perked up a little as she warmed to her subject. "Sarah lives above the shop. I'll call her and tell her you're coming in with some clothes. I think you'll like her."

So here I was, scouring for a parking spot on the narrow street off Michigan Avenue, trying to get as close to the shop as I could and wondering how in blue blazes I was going to lug the boxes from the car. Maybe Sarah Everett had a cart or a dolly or... *something*. I carefully parallel-parked and was piling out when the door to the little shop flew open.

"Get your sorry ass out of here and don't ever show your face in my shop again, y'all hear me?" A tiny redhead stood in the doorway shouting at the man who'd stumbled out the door ahead of her. He was at least three times her size, and yet he was practically cowering. "If you so much as look in the window again, I'm callin' the cops, ya got that?" Her strident voice carried down the street practically to Michigan Avenue.

The man backed away from her, his hands open and raised. He said something I didn't hear.

The little fireball practically spat at him. "Don't you dare say another word, jackass. You just keep movin'!"

She turned and caught sight of me, watching with apparent interest as I stacked one box on top of another and walked her direction. "Lock that vehicle or it'll be gone when you get back out." She marched back into the shop.

I aimed the remote at the car and waited for two chirps before I headed toward the old brownstone building. The area didn't really seem all that bad—a little old and rundown, but not the ghetto, by any means. I bumped the shop's door open with my butt, and as I stepped inside the warm interior, someone took the boxes from me.

"You must be Carrie's friend." The redhead set the boxes on the floor next to a glass case and gave me a grin.

"I am." I extended my hand, feeling like an Amazon next to her. "Julianne Miles. Julie."

"I'm Sarah Everett." She shook firmly, her tiny hand engulfed in mine. "I recognized the car." She nodded to the boxes. "Is this everything?"

"No, I've still got two more boxes and three garment bags in the car."

"Good God, woman, did you bring everything you own?" Atlanta was evident in her accent, but she didn't have a deep drawl, barely a hint of the old South.

"Seems like it, doesn't it?" I couldn't help grinning back; her smile was infectious. I was trying to make this gracious woman work with the tough broad I'd seen only moments before.

My confusion must have shown on my face because Sarah threw back her head and laughed a rich delicious sound. "I'm not usually the hard ass you saw out on the street. But these butt-wipes come in here searching for their wives or girlfriends—the women they've been beating the crap out of—and they think I'm going to tell them where the poor chickies are? Fat chance of that." She leaned over the counter. "Holly! I'm gonna go help with some boxes, get out here and man the register."

"Is he gone?" A very large black girl came out between the louvered doors behind the counter, timidly peeking around.

"Of course he's gone, sweetie, and he ain't comin' back, so unbunch your panties." Sarah held her hand out, indicating for me to go through the door ahead of her, then followed me out to the Prius, talking animatedly as we walked. "That poor gal is scared shitless of any man that even passes by. I get it, we've all been there, but she needs to toughen up. She can't be hidin' in La Belle Femme the rest of her life."

"Was that guy after her?" I asked, opening the trunk on the Prius and handing Sarah a carton.

"Nope, but she's scared of anything with a pecker. She got worked over pretty good a couple months ago. Just got the wires taken out of her jaw last week." Sarah looked askance at my shocked expression, but changed the subject as we each carried a box and the garment bags to the shop. "So what brings you here? Chicago in the dead of winter ain't no vacation."

"I'm taking a break for a while." I wouldn't meet her frank stare.

"Gettin' away from all the memories of your dead husband?" Obviously Sarah Everett went for the blunt question.

I had to appreciate that about her because I was once that way myself. I nodded briefly.

"Sorry about that." Sincere sympathy showed in her hazel eyes.

"Thanks." I smiled, probably a little wanly. "I miss him every day."

"Yeah? Well, nice you got one of the good ones." Sarah shoved open the door and held it with her backside as I walked through it. "Too bad it couldn't have my ex—he's still roamin' the streets."

"Charlie *was* one of the good ones." I put the box on the counter and hung the garment bags on a rack nearby. I let my gaze roam the charming shop. Racks of dresses, suits, and blouses filled the big high-ceilinged room painted a soft sage green. Shelves of shoes lined the wall opposite a huge display window that let in streams of bright January sun. A white wicker settee and chairs and a table were placed cozily in the center of the room on a big delicately designed oriental rug. I could see dressing rooms on the back wall, curtained off with chintz. Ferns hung from chains in the window and a spider plant overflowed on a stand near the wicker. The ambiance was feminine, elegant, and homey all at once. "This is lovely."

"Thanks." Sarah dropped her box on the floor and hung the garment bag next to mine. "It's been a long haul and funding's always an issue, which is why we appreciate Carrie's hard work so much." She glanced around. "Holly?"

The young woman popped her head up from where she'd been kneeling by the shoe wall. "Yes, ma'am?"

"What are you doing?"

"Finding some shoes for Jeanie." Holly stood up with a couple of pairs of black shoes in her hands. "She's trying on an outfit for her interview tomorrow." She motioned toward the dressing area.

A young woman pulled aside the curtain in the first cubicle and stepped out onto the carpet in bare feet. She was dressed in a gray skirt and jacket with a pink blouse that tied at the neck in a bow. The skirt was mid-calf length and the boxy jacket had shoulder pads. The total effect was as if her grandmother had dressed her sometime in the eighties. She seemed right on the edge of bursting into tears.

"Looks real good." Sarah walked toward the woman, who was pretty in a low-key kind of way as she turned slowly in front a three-way mirror. Sarah went up behind her and pulled her long chestnut hair off her shoulders and held it back. "You need to tidy this hair, some, Jeanie." She scraped the hair into a loose, low ponytail and secured it with a hair band that she had around her wrist. "There… very professional."

Jeanie reminded me of a cornered rabbit. Her gray eyes were huge and she stood, shoulders hunched and uncomfortable, in front of the mirror.

Sarah glanced back at me. "What do you think?" She took a pair of low black pumps from Holly and tossed them down in front of Jeanie. "Here, darlin', slip into these."

I walked slowly back to the rear of the shop as Sarah turned Jeanie around to face me. "Good, huh?" She quirked a brow.

"If she's applying for a job at a convent." I immediately regretted the comment. Sarah was trying to help this poor terrified creature and sure didn't need any kibitzing from me. I opened my mouth to apologize as Sarah grimaced and Jeanie turned away, clearly chagrined. She stared at the mirror again, tears shimmering in her eyes.

I closed my eyes briefly and shook my head. "Sorry, Sarah. I don't mean she doesn't look fine… but—" I felt incredibly foolish. "Sorry, it's not my business." I finished with a lame shrug.

"So, what do *you* suggest?" Sarah gave me a cool stare as she crossed her arms and tilted her head.

I shrugged again.

Sarah nodded. "No, seriously. Tell us what's wrong. You're the big fashion model."

Jeanie turned around. "You're a fashion model?"

"I was once… not anymore." I wanted to bolt. Carrie must have filled Sarah in more than she'd let on earlier. "I'm going to let you get back to work." I backed away, bumping into a rack of blouses. "S—sorry… Nice to meet you… "

"No." Sarah caught my arm and gave me a lopsided grin. "I get bristly. It's not you. We really *could* use some advice. Frankly,

I don't have an ounce of fashion sense. One of the few things old dickhead never could beat into me." She winked as Jeanie and Holly both snickered. "Help us out, okay?"

I released a hesitant breath, my hands curling into fists at my side, and tried to decide how honest I could be. Sarah asked for advice, but was it fair for me to take the poor kid apart? However, I knew exactly what would work for her and probably give her the confidence she needed. I glanced at the three of them clearly waiting for whatever gems of fashion wisdom I would impart and decided to go for broke. "Um… okay. First of all, never, ever that shade of pale pink unless you're younger than twelve or older than seventy."

"Really?" Sarah's brows rose.

I gazed thoughtfully at Jeanie, standing there in front of the three-way, lost in that boxy jacket. Holly lurked around the edges as though she anticipated trouble, but Sarah gave me an expectant smile.

"Hang on." I trotted up to the front of the shop to my bags and boxes and rummaged through a couple.

Jeanie appeared to be about a size six, although she wasn't quite as tall as me. I tugged open a carton and sorted through it until I found a simple white silk blouse. Then I unzipped a garment bag and pulled out jackets and skirts and dresses. *Ah ha!* The brown tweed suit was the next-to-last item I pulled out—a simple brown and golden tweed jacket with a matching slim pencil skirt. The color would bring out the gold highlights in Jeanie's hair and the jacket was short and fitted—perfect for her slim figure. The skirt might be a little long, but we could hem it in no time.

I marched the clothes back to her. "Here, try this and tuck in the blouse."

Jeanie peered apprehensively at Sarah, seeking permission.

Sarah nodded brusquely. "Get in there and put it on, girl."

I hurried over to the shoe wall with Holly close on my heels. "What size?"

"Six and a half." Holly pointed to the appropriate section of the shoe display and I scanned the rows of pumps, flats, and kitten heels. I pulled a pair of brown suede pumps from the rack and held them up.

"What do you think, Sarah?"

She nodded approval.

I peeked inside. Tory Burch—nice shoes. I passed them to Holly. "Accessories? Like scarves?"

Holly led the way to the front of the store where scarves were attractively displayed from loops on a rack. I sorted through them, finally selecting a long, wide scarf in a deep gold, rust, and brown pattern. Rubbing the fabric between my fingers, I grinned at Sarah. "This is silk. And gorgeous. See how rich these colors are." I shook it out and saw the square capital letters along one side. "Fendi! Sarah, you really do run a designer shop."

"Names don't mean much to me, but yeah, we get a lot of expensive stuff in here. Most of our donations come from women with bucks, thanks to your friend Carrie's influence."

I scurried back to the rear of the store as Jeanie was coming out of the dressing room. Stopping her, I lifted my arms, preparing to loop the silk piece around her neck a couple of times. With a screech and a sharp intake of breath, she threw her hands up and backed away. I glanced over my shoulder at Sarah, who hustled up next to the girl.

"Jeanie, she's not going to hurt you. It's an accessory… a pretty extra for the outfit." Sarah put her hand out and I laid the silk material in her palm. She held it out to Jeanie, who was practically cowering near the dressing cubicle. "See? Why don't *you* put it on and Julie can tell you how to fix it, okay?"

Trembling, Jeanie reached for the scarf and hung it over her neck before straightening her shoulders and moving to the three-way mirror.

What in God's holy name had happened to this poor creature?

I stood a yard or so behind her in the mirror and gave her instructions on how to loop the scarf. At last, she stood reflected three times in the mirror and each one was elegant, poised, and lovely. She turned this way and that until a small smile broke through the sad facade.

"You're perfect!" Holly clapped her hands while Sarah nodded, her eyes shining approval.

"Do you think it's okay?" Jeanie's voice was as soft as I'd expected it to be, and my heart ached at the tremulous smile she gave me.

"You look like a million bucks, honey." My fingers itched to do something else with her hair.

"What about her hair?" Sarah must have been reading my mind.

"It's gorgeous. So thick and shiny. I'd say, let's take the curling iron to it and let it tumble over her shoulders loose and natural." I approached Jeanie with caution, locking eyes with her in the mirror. "May I?"

She nodded, but I could see a hint of uncertainty in her expression. Very gingerly, I unwound the band and fluffed her hair out over her shoulders. "We could maybe use a barrette or something and secure one side. Or better, let's tuck it behind your ears, like this." I demonstrated. Her hair was heavy. It felt like spun silk in my fingers, and as I combed through it I could feel her shoulders relaxing. "You're lovely, Jeanie, very professional," I whispered, my voice catching in my throat.

"Holly, why don't you and Jeanie go up front and find a pair of earrings—something small and gold would be right, don't you think, Julie?" Sarah's eyes sent a subtle signal, so I nodded and turned Jeanie away from the mirror with a quick shoulder squeeze. She followed Holly to the jewelry counter.

"What happened to her?" I was almost afraid to ask, but I had to know.

"Her husband used to tie her to the bedposts with scarves or neckties and rape her, then beat the crap out of her when he was done." Sarah's voice held no emotion whatsoever, but her sad eyes said it all. "She came into the shelter so battered and bruised, you couldn't even see the true color of her eyes."

"Oh, God." I glanced over my shoulder at the two of them giggling over a tray of earrings. "How do you survive something like that?" I kept my voice quiet.

"You do it because you know you have no other choice," she answered softly. "And one day, you know you can't survive another moment in hell, so you find the strength to leave."

The power in her voice touched something deep inside me and suddenly I struggled with a sick feeling of guilt. How insane, how selfish I'd been for almost a year, weeping and feeling sorry for myself when women like Jeanie and Holly and Sarah had suffered so much more pain than I'd ever known in my life.

I touched Sarah's shoulder. "I want to help. Tell me how I can help."

CHAPTER 6

I was fairly bubbling with enthusiasm as I set plates on the counter for Will and me in Carrie and Liam's kitchen. The change in me was so dramatic I almost had to keep checking the mirror to see if it was really me. Working at the shelter had brought new purpose to my life and I hopped out of bed each morning ready to go. What a difference from when I'd arrived over a month ago.

Will sat on a barstool, watching me bustle around the kitchen, tossing a salad, cleaning asparagus, and checking the chicken baking in the oven. I was talking a mile a minute, but he didn't seem to mind. He simply sat, wearing an enigmatic smile. I imagine he couldn't believe I was the same sad quiet Julie who'd arrived several weeks earlier.

We'd gotten past that awkward night when we kissed, mostly because Will insisted on it. If I'd had my way after that humiliation, we'd only have nodded to one another as we passed in the elevator or at the mailboxes. But he kept inserting himself into my life at every opportunity, and tonight, I was glad for his company. However I was still determined to keep things between us strictly casual.

I knew it irritated him that I never missed a chance to treat him like one of my sons, even to the point of offering him cookies and milk one night when he showed up at my apartment with *Tracy and Hepburn, The Definitive Collection* on DVD. Hell, I even tried to sew a button on for him when a shirt had come back from the cleaners missing one, and he'd dropped by to borrow a needle and thread. It was a defense mechanism, and the fact that I felt compelled to use it worried me some. Did that mean I was more drawn to him than I was willing to admit?

The man *was* incredibly attractive— intelligent, easy to talk to, warm, and funny. He could charm the socks right off any woman he wanted, so why had he chosen to spend time with me? I'd made it very clear that I couldn't get involved with him, but he seemed content with simply hanging out as buddies. We watched movies, met for coffee in the mornings, and ordered in take-out a few nights. He even joined me in the pool in the mornings, swimming laps with a long, loose-limbed stroke.

But sometimes I caught him gazing at me, and the look in his eyes was way more than friendly. I'd opened up a can of worms that night with that kiss, and I wasn't at all sure how to close it. The difference in our ages wasn't truly my biggest issue; it was just a convenient excuse. No, my problem was Charlie. Even though he'd been gone over a year, I was still good and married. Menopausal horniness aside, no other man—not even one as kind and interesting as Will Brody—would ever have my heart.

Charlie was with me. I felt him near all the time. I knew he approved of my moving to Chicago for the winter, and I sensed his support of my volunteering at the shelter. It would be exactly the kind of thing he would do. Charlie was a philanthropist—he'd donated time to the free clinic in Traverse City, and he was one of the few cardiac surgeons who operated on uninsured patients for free, which always had him in hot water with the other docs in his practice.

Some nights, I talked to him, telling him about my day at the shelter or my visit to the new therapist or even that I'd found a new restaurant or an interesting shop. I could pretend he was just a few steps away in the bathroom or changing in the closet. When I was alone, I drew comfort from my memories and the sense that he'd always be near me. The therapist said it was perfectly normal to think, *Oh, I'll have to tell Charlie about this,* or, *Wouldn't Charlie think this was hilarious?* After being with someone for over thirty years, wanting to share your life with them was natural. But Dr. Jardin also encouraged me to find new friends, so that's exactly what I was doing with Sarah Everett, the other volunteers at the shelter, and of course, Will Brody.

I poured Riesling into wine glasses and set one in front of him. "Found this at the wine shop over by the law school. I hope it's decent. Rieslings can sometimes be too sweet." We both sipped and I nodded approval. "Not too bad, huh? I tried to find Tuckaway. It was Charlie's favorite and really yummy."

"Tuckaway?" He took another sip of the wine and cocked his head. "Are you talking about the winery in the Sierra foothills in California?"

"Mm hm, the town is called Angels Camp. I only remember that because I loved the name. I've never been to the winery, but *he* went whenever he had conferences in San Francisco. He always had it shipped since we couldn't get it in Michigan. I'm guessing you can't get it here, either." I took another drink before adding the asparagus to the simmering water. "I should check their website."

"You should. I've actually been there. Liam and I used to go wine tasting when we were in California. Tuckaway is a great winery."

"Charlie loved their Riesling and their petit Syrah." I bent over to open the oven door to check the chicken and set the loaf of bread on the rack next to it while I was down there. When I shut the oven door, I shook my hair back off my flushed face. "Almost. Just about five more minutes and everything will be ready." I sat down next to him, one fuzzy slipper hanging precariously off my toe.

"So things are working for you at the shop?" His voice was a little strained, and he was focusing intently on my face—a trick I'd seen too many men use when what they really wanted was to stare at my breasts.

Maybe this blue, wide-necked sweater was a mistake tonight, but it was one of my favorites and I'd gained back enough weight that it had finally stopped sagging on me. I ignored his expression and went for the question. "I love it. Sarah and the girls are so sweet and dedicated and I can see why. I haven't heard everyone's story yet, but the ones I have heard are horrific. The men they were involved with were pure evil."

"Really?" At last I had his attention. "Like how?"

"Well, every one of them was physically abusive in some wretched way, but also emotionally and mentally. They tore these poor women down to the point that most of them truly hate themselves. There's a group therapy session at the shelter and even some of the women who no longer stay there come back for it." I rose again to check on the asparagus. "And these are intelligent, educated women from good backgrounds—one of them is a nurse and one's an attorney, whose husband was a judge. He used to make her lick his shoes."

"Jesus!" Will's eyes widened. "Seriously?"

"Yep." When I nodded, my hair brushed my neck and bare shoulders. "And that's not the worst thing I've heard. God bless them all, their stories are nightmares. I don't know how they did it… or why."

"I've never gotten that, either. Why do women stay in circumstances like that anyway? Why don't they just leave?"

"Sarah told me these situations take years to build up. That the men work hard to gain the women's trust and love, and then tear them down bit by bit. They convince them they're worthless and not worthy of anyone's love. These guys are real nutjobs, but they're also often quite charismatic. And it doesn't matter how much education you have, when you've had your mind messed with at the level these guys do it, your self-confidence and ability to discern reality go in the toilet."

"God, that's frightening."

"Isn't it? Sarah comes from a very prominent family in Georgia. Her ex is some big real estate mogul down there, but he treated her like a dog and I'm not being metaphorical. He used to put a leash on her when they were in bed." I shut my eyes at the memory of Sarah's story, which I'd heard one night after we'd closed the shelter and opened the bottle of tequila Sarah kept in her desk drawer.

"That sounds really grim, Julie."

"It's not." I shook my head. "I mean... the stories *are* grim, but the women are so amazing. They come in completely defeated, and by the time they leave, they're ready to face the world on their own. It's inspiring."

"What does the therapist say about you being there so much?" Will reached for the bottle of wine and refilled both our glasses.

"She's all for it." I got the chicken and bread out of the oven, wrapped the bread in a towel and covered the chicken breasts with a piece of foil to let them rest for a few minutes. "I think she wants me to see that even though I've had tragedy in my life, other people have too. It's not only making me doubly grateful for what a wonderful husband Charlie was, but I'm pretty much over feeling sorry for myself."

"You do seem happier." Will's grin warmed me right down to my toes. His eyes narrowed as a flush warmed my cheeks. I knew he could see the dangerous effect he was having, and I wished I was better at hiding my reactions. Instead, I stepped back.

"I *am* happier, and I had a great idea last night for another fundraiser for the shelter. When I mentioned it to Sarah today, she was all about it."

Color rose up his neck, too, and he started to say something. The words wouldn't come, so he gulped down the wine, then cleared his throat. "What's that?"

"I was thinking that it would be fun to do a fashion show. You know, using clothes that have been donated to Belle Femme. I'm sure I could get some of my model friends to help out. At first, I suggested using women from the shelter as models. I thought it'd be a kick for them, but Sarah nixed that idea."

"Why? I bet they'd have fun."

"She was afraid of the publicity—that maybe the women's exes would see them in a newspaper picture or TV feature or something. I get that." When I shrugged, the sweater, which had a wide loose neckline, fell to one side, revealing a glimpse of my collarbone and shoulder. Hastily, I rearranged it, wondering again if I should've selected something less revealing to wear tonight.

Will gave a little sigh and got up from his stool, jiggling change in his pocket as he wandered around the kitchen like a nervous cat. The laptop was set up and open on the wooden surface of the table by the window. He picked the little optical USB mouse beside it, turning it over in his fingers.

I caught his smile. "Hey, kid, no making fun of an old timer who can't handle a track pad, okay?"

"I didn't say anything." He raised both hands in self-defense. "I'm glad to see you got the wireless going."

"You didn't have to say anything. I caught the smirk." I scooped poached asparagus onto our plates next to slices of baked chicken. "And don't start congratulating me yet. I still haven't figured out the damn wireless, so I can't get on the Internet. I've been emailing the kids from the shop. There's always downtime and Sarah told me to feel free to check for messages if I felt like it." I rolled my eyes. "That's all I ever use the computer for anyway. But I really *would* like to get this one working so I can use it to map out plans for the fashion show and to email my friends from the agency. That's Charlie's old laptop, but I can get to my own email with webmail."

"I'll take a look after dinner, okay?"

"Dinner's ready." I waved my hands like a magician over the spread on the countertop. "Come and get it."

CHAPTER 7

Dinner was delicious. Cooking had always brought me pleasure and it was nice to have someone to cook for again. Not that I intended to be making meals for Will Brody on a regular basis, but I had to admit it was good to be in the kitchen and using my creative skills. As we ate and chatted about the neighborhood, his work, the latest emails from my family, and the shop, I was suddenly conscious of how at ease I could be with him. The attraction simmering just below the surface didn't have to make things awkward. We could do this if we both simply kept things in perspective. Friends—relaxed and easy.

But it also occurred to me that I'd spent most of the evening talking about myself and the shop and my kids. With news of Kevin and Meg's due date coming up, the fashion show fundraiser, and Renee's latest email from Africa, the conversation had centered on *my* life. I knew very little about Will, while he knew my whole history.

I reached for the wine and added some to both our glasses. "Tell me about you, Will."

"What about me?" One blond brow rose. "I'm good. Just

lining up some dates for Liam's summer tour and getting his tax information together."

"No, I mean personal stuff like, where were you born? Do you have any siblings? Have you ever been married?" I smiled. "I hardly know anything about you except you were once a stock-broker. Carrie sent me a link to a very nice *Wall Street Journal* article. The *Sorcerer of LaSalle Street*, huh?"

"No way she sent you that old article." He bowed his head as a blush reddened his cheeks, then he shrugged, a little self-depre-cating movement of muscle under his gray Northwestern fleece hoodie.

"Yup. Very impressive. Why'd you quit?" I was enjoying his discomfort. He was a great one for asking questions. Now he could answer some.

"It was time." He eyed me, as though gauging what he wanted to reveal. "I was just out of a marriage that had bored itself to death. Had plenty of money. Figured out that working 24/7 wasn't what I wanted to do anymore. About that time, I met Liam. Being his financial advisor and then his manager sounded like a kick. The rest is history."

"What's the rest?"

"There's not a lot more to tell. I'm from Fremont, California. Went to UC Davis. Got my MBA from Northwestern and decided to stay in Chicago after graduation. Two sisters and a brother. My parents still live in the house I grew up in. I started working with Liam about eight years ago." He raised his palms in a *that's all* gesture.

"Come on, Will. I want some serious scoop now." I gave his foot a playful nudge with my toe.

"*You* come on, Jules. I'm no good at talking about myself. I'm not very interesting." His color deepened and sweat appeared on the side of his face in spite of the cool air from the ceiling fan over the table a few feet away. He *really* was uncomfortable.

That made me cringe. I searched for a way to put him back at ease. "Okay then, want to play a game with me?"

"What kind of a game?" Will's tone was cautious.

"It's one that my mom used to play with her patients." I leaned toward him. "I did tell you my mom was a psychologist before she died, right?"

"No, but that explains a lot!" He grinned. "So now we're going to play amateur psychoanalyst, huh? Do I have lie down for this?" He leered—or at least he tried to. No way was Will Brody ever going to do dirty old man convincingly.

"No, you dope. Mom did this so her patients would be more comfortable and open up. It's a getting-to-know-you thing."

"We already know each other."

"This is just for fun." I gave him my best little pout, the one that always worked on Charlie when I wanted to do something and he was reluctant. "Come on."

Will gave me a dubious gaze then sighed. "Okay, what do we do?"

"We tell each other six obscure facts about ourselves, but make one a lie and then we each try to figure out which one's the lie." I explained. "You start."

"Six obscure facts?" Will's blue eyes narrowed. "Hm… give me a minute. I'm going to have to come up with six things you don't already know about me."

"I don't think that'll be hard, Will. You haven't been all that revealing in the past few weeks."

"Six things… let me think here." He leaned his elbow on the bar and rested his chin in his palm. After a long moment, he said, "Okay, here we go. Number one—I love baseball, but I quit little league when I was seven because the coach told me I ran like a girl. Two—I play the guitar like James Taylor. Three—I didn't have my first date until I was eighteen. Four—I broke my arm surfing when I was fifteen." He paused again, glancing thoughtfully at the ceiling and then continued. "Five—I've performed in ballets with Ballet San Jose and Chicago Ballet. Six—I always take two showers a day—one in the morning and one at night." He nodded with satisfaction, apparently quite pleased with himself.

"Wow, you did that really well. I'm impressed."

"You should be. It was an effort." Will smirked. "Now which one's the lie?"

"It's a coin toss, my friend, between the ballet thing and the guitar, but I'm thinking there's no way you play the guitar like James Taylor—that's the lie."

He stared at me in mock dismay. "Well, that's a crappy assumption to make. Why do you think that's the lie?"

"First, nobody plays the guitar like James Taylor except James Taylor, and besides you're too young to be a Taylor fan," I replied, impressed with my own unerring logic.

"Ha! You'd be wrong, Slugger! Thanks to my mom, I'm a huge James Taylor fan. I even met him a few years ago when he played the reunion concert with Carole King at the Troubadour in LA. Dad took all of us down for Mom's birthday."

"Okay, you're a fan, but I'm still sticking with my first assessment—I don't believe you play the guitar. It doesn't fit with geeky MBA thing and besides, I've never once seen you with a guitar."

He shook his head. "Wrong again. I've been playing the guitar since I was thirteen. I have four guitars in the spare room at my place, including a very nice antique Alvarez acoustic that used to belong to my grandfather. I even sound-proofed the walls of my apartment so I can rock out whenever I feel like it." He jerked a thumb in the general direction of his apartment. "Pops taught me how to play… and seriously, a guy my age being into music from the sixties and seventies is pretty damn geeky."

"Are you kidding me?" I was shocked. "Why have you not

mentioned this—you've never even alluded to playing the guitar, ever... not in all the time I've known you."

"You've only known me a few weeks and a little mystery is a good thing." Will crossed his arms over his chest. "I jam with a group of guys I met when I was in grad school. We get together every other Saturday and play all day."

I was stumped. Here was a side of Will Brody I'd never imagined. What else did I not know about this man? I knew he kissed like a champ—I certainly did know that. I swallowed hard and sent that thought out the door. "Then it has to be the ballet thing." I returned Will's smile, feeling a little flutter low in my belly.

"Nope."

"Oh, come on, Will!" I rolled my eyes and shoved my hair behind my ear. "No way have you ever been in a ballet!"

"Do you know what a supernumerary is?" Will stacked his salad plate onto his empty dinner plate.

"A fun word you just made up?"

"No, a *supernumerary* is an extra, like someone who does a walk-on part. In the ballet, the supers are like human stage props. My sister, Tessa, worked in the costume shop at Ballet San Jose, so she recruited me and my brother to be supers." I could see it in his eyes. He was dead serious. "Then when I moved here, I saw a call from the Chicago Ballet for supers on a board at Northwestern, so I went and auditioned. I guess I've been in the *Nutcracker* six times and in *Romeo and Juliet* and *Swan Lake* and others. Last time was about five years ago before I became Liam's manager." His stern expression dared me to challenge him.

I snorted a laugh. "Do you wear a tights and a tutu?"

"Okay, now see? *This* is why we've never had this conversation. Besides you're still oh-for-six, Ms. Miles—only four choices left and *I'm* making a new rule—three guesses only. You've got one more shot."

"Don't get all huffy! I'd hate for you to bust a seam in your tights." I simply couldn't stop chuckling.

Will gazed at me in mock severity, shaking his head. "I never should have told you about the ballet. Doomed myself to months of tacky tutu jokes, have I?"

"Most likely *years*." I swallowed my giggles and sat up straighter, trying to assume a more serious stance. "Okay, okay. Let me think for a minute—you seriously distracted me with the whole ballet thing." Truth was, I was picturing him, gorgeous in tights and a tunic, and the picture was causing my blood pressure to rise. Heat suffused my cheeks, so I took a sip of the cold wine. "Only one more shot? I guess… I don't believe you didn't have your first date until you were eighteen. That's a little hard to buy even though you told me what a nerd you thought you were."

"Ha!" Will clasped his hands over his head in triumph. "You blew it. The lie was I broke my arm surfing. I've never even been on a surfboard. What do I win?"

"Now, see? That was the one that was easiest to believe since you grew up in California—oh, and the running like a girl thing, I bought that immediately." I winked at him.

"Thanks a bunch. Okay, your six things, please. I'm on a roll, I'm sure *I'll* get *your* lie on the first guess." He swiveled on the stool and his knee bumped mine, setting off a few small fireworks inside me.

I should've moved my leg away from his.

But I didn't.

His muscled thigh against mine felt too good. Instead I gave him my sassiest grin and flirted shamelessly. "First, can we talk about the two showers a day? That's a little quirky, don't you think? You've never mentioned the OCD before."

"That's not OCD." A brow rose. "And it's not all about being a clean freak, either. The nighttime shower is for relaxing at the end of the day." He pointed, his finger just inches from my nose. "Hey, stop stalling! Six things, lady… now."

"Oh, all right!" I tried to assume a distressed expression, but failed miserably. "Okay, number one—I broke my nose three times before I turned five. Number two—I was valedictorian of my high school class. Number three—I never learned to ride a bike. Number four—when Charlie and I went to Italy the first time, I accidentally asked a man in Cortona if he wanted to taste my toes." I stopped as he chortled. "Did I interrupt your list with rude laughter?"

"No, no you didn't. I'm sorry. Please, continue." Will closed his lips tight, but merriment shone in his eyes.

"Number five—the first time I shaved my legs, Mom had to take me to the emergency room. Number six—five years ago, I dropped Charlie's car keys over Niagara Falls because when I'm at the top of someplace really high, I have an irresistible urge to throw something off."

"My God, I'm speechless." His eyes widened as he raked his fingers through his hair, leaving it standing up in spiky tufts. "I don't even know where to begin."

"Three guesses, my little *cygnet*, or it's a draw."

"Ah, a cheap *Swan Lake* reference." He sighed theatrically. "So it begins."

"Yup," I agreed. "Guess the lie, Will."

"Okay, I think the lie is—" he narrowed his eyes and pursed his lips, "—that you were valedictorian of your high school class. But not because I don't think that's possible, I do. I really do." He backpedaled, trying to gauge my reactions. "I only picked that one because I want the others to be true. I can't stop picturing you asking some old Italian guy on the street to lick your toes, and the rest of them have such great story potential, I'd hate for them to be lies. I want to hear more."

"I do *not* believe this." I tapped his forearm with a closed fist.

"I got it?" Will grinned with triumph. "I won. Cool."

"You got it. How did you do that?"

I shoved the stool away from the bar and rose to take our dishes to the sink. I was antsy sitting in such close quarters with him, with the fresh male scent of him wafting across the foot or so of distance between us. Was this dinner a huge mistake? Was I going to spend the rest of my time in Chicago lusting after a man who was way too young for me? And drowning in guilt?

"It was just the one I didn't want to be true, honest." His laughter filled the room, and in spite of the steam rising from the sink, I shivered at the effect he was having on me. "But right now, I want details of all the other stuff—starting with the guy in Italy."

CHAPTER 8

Will futzed with Charlie's laptop—*my* laptop—while I cleaned up the kitchen and kept him amused with the stories of a near toe-tasting in Cortona and tossing Charlie's car keys over Niagara Falls. Will howled at my stories and teased me gently about my obvious inability to speak Italian. A few clicks, a moment of tapping on the keyboard, and magically, he was online.

"How'd you do that?" I dried my hands on a clean tea towel and peeked at the screen over his shoulder. "I did exactly what Javier told me to do and I couldn't get it to work."

"It's a gift." He flashed me a grin full of beautiful white teeth that sent a rush of sensation straight through me. "I could be your own personal guru." Those blue, blue eyes offered way more than computer advice.

"Yeah? Bet that'll cost me." I tossed him a wink.

What was it about this man that hyped up my flirting mechanism? I assumed it had died with Charlie, or if it hadn't died, it was in mothballs at this stage. But here I was, smiling coyly and leaning over his shoulder.

"Oh, we could probably work out some suitable arrangement," he replied. "I might not be cheap, but I'm certainly reasonable."

Will's handsome face was mere inches from mine. I could smell the citrus shampoo he used and the wine he'd had with dinner. My nipples tightened as my breasts brushed his broad back.

Uh-oh. The heat radiating through me told me I was teetering on the edge of real trouble. I couldn't believe I was so attracted to this guy. But I was also determined to keep the promise I'd made to myself after that humiliating night a few weeks earlier. I definitely needed to watch my step with Will Brody.

I turned my attention to the screen in front of him. "Um, thanks for doing this, Will. It'll be nice to be able to get on the Internet here at home. I can stop checking email at the shop."

"Okay, let's take a look." With an obvious sigh, he clicked the email icon on the desktop before I could stop him. The program began to load. "God, you've got a ton of new email. I thought you said you were checking it at the shop."

"Oh, no wait." I put my hand on top of Will's on the mouse. "That's not my email, it's probably Charlie's old hospital account. I have to use webmail on this computer."

"Well, so far we've downloaded thirty-seven emails and they're still coming." Will pointed to the box racking up the message count, but at the same time, moved his fingers under mine on the mouse. "Want to just let it do its thing? I can open the browser for you to get to your webmail while it's downloading. Then if you like, I can delete his account and set up *your* email for you."

"Um… I guess." My pulse was quickening under the gentle massaging action of his thumb on my wrist. But at the same time, my curiosity was piqued about the emails pouring into Charlie's inbox. Surely the hospital should have closed out his account by now. Will clicked on the browser and the new window covered the email program, but I could see the little counter in the taskbar, still showing emails coming in.

"When's the last time you checked this email box, Julie?" Will glanced up at me, his brows furrowed. He gently tugged his hand from mine as a pinging alert sent him back to the email program. It was done.

Good lord, 1,092 new messages.

"I've *never* checked it before—this was Charlie's laptop. I brought it along with me because I couldn't find the charger for mine and his was all together in one bag. Plus, it's newer and nicer than mine."

I tossed the towel on the countertop behind me and pulled a chair around to peer at the screen with Will. The inbox list was stuffed with emails, the last one dated yesterday, a year and month after Charlie had died. Will scrolled through the list, stopping at one from Tuck-away Winery—most likely an ad or something. As far as I could see, there wasn't anything there related to cardiology or the hospital.

My God, this is Charlie's personal email.

Why had it never even occurred to me that Charlie might have a separate personal email box? When the kids emailed me, they'd always copied Charlie at the hospital. He never mentioned having a personal email. I tried to think back, but I couldn't place a time when I'd seen Charlie use this computer at home. He'd always put it in his office with strict instructions to leave it alone. Will's finger twitched on the mouse button.

Unnatural cold clutched in the pit of my stomach and I grabbed his hand. "Close this out, Will. It isn't any of our business."

"*What?*" Will's eyes widened as he gave a snort of disbelief. "*Why?*"

"It feels wrong to go through his private email. It'd be like reading his journal or something. Charlie and I respected each other's privacy. Hell, I never even opened his wallet without asking him first."

"Really? Aren't you even a little curious?"

"No. Close the program, okay?" My tone had an edge that I immediately regretted, but I couldn't explain my reluctance. I simply did *not* want to peruse those emails.

"Okay." With a concerned glance in my direction, he clicked out of the program.

"I'm sorry." I searched for the right words as he sat patiently, one hand on the keyboard. He deserved an explanation if for no other reason than because I snapped at him. "I–I just can't face that right now. I'm so much better, you know? And it'd be like sticking your tongue in a sore tooth to see if it still hurts. Probing into the past, reading those emails and seeing what interested him besides me and the kids and his work would only open up the healing places."

"I get it, Jules. You don't have to apologize." He closed the laptop and stood up. "But if you want me to set it up for your email, I can go in and add it to the program."

"Thanks, but I think I'll stick with the webmail for now." When I caught Will's eye, he was staring at me, confusion evident on his handsome face. So I gave him a big smile. "I appreciate you hooking me up." I extended one hand toward the kitchen. "How 'bout dessert? It's chocolate molten lava cake from that bakery by the shop. Have you ever had it?"

I warmed the chocolate cake in the microwave, then added hot fudge and whipped cream before I put it in front of him with flourish.

"Ta da!" I handed him a fork. The extra hot fudge and whipped cream were my idea. "Sarah introduced me to these wicked things, she calls 'em a mountain of sin on a plate and she is *so* right." A mischievous little devil took over and I gave him a coy smile. "Carrie and I have our own special term for desserts like this."

"Really? What is it?" He poured rich red zinfandel into glasses. I'd opened it when I got out the dessert because red wine always tasted great with chocolate.

"UFOs."

"What?"

"We call them UFOs." I flipped my hair back with a slight head toss.

"UFO? What's it stand for?"

"Guess." God, I was flirting again. Elbows on the countertop, I rested my chin in my palm as an impish smile played on my lips. This guy brought out the naughty in me like no one else had but Charlie. I straightened up, trying to recover some semblance of propriety.

"I'm not a good guesser," he said. "'Fess up, okay?"

"Um… no." I turned and pulled open a drawer behind me. Silverware rattled as I rummaged. "I think I'll let you give it some thought."

"Oh, come on, Julie. You're the one who brought it up, so tell me."

"Nope, I don't think you're old enough." It was the old defense, but at the moment, it was all I had. I gestured to the plate in front of him. "Eat. Go on before it gets cold."

"Where's yours?" He glanced around, but there was only one serving of molten lava cake. "Do I have to eat this in front of you?"

I produced another fork from behind my back. "No silly, you have to *share* it with me."

"You obviously aren't a serious chocolate lover, Ms. Miles." He stuck his fork into the cake and scooped out a huge bite covered in fluffy whipped cream.

"Excuse me?" I got my own forkful of chocolate decadence

from the other side of the plate. "I happen to be a world-class chocolate lover, Mr. Brody." The cake practically melted in my mouth, chocolaty and velvety smooth. I took a sip of the zin. The combination of chocolate and red wine was incredible.

"I beg to differ." He took another big bite of cake, the expression on his face one of utter delight. "A real chocolate lover would never share or expect anyone else to."

I licked chocolate sauce and whipped cream from my lips. "You couldn't be more wrong. A true chocolate lover *always* shares because we know how important it is that everyone have the opportunity to know this kind of deliciousness." I winked. "My boy, never ever try to best a menopausal woman when it comes to chocolate. Didn't your momma ever teach you that?"

He grimaced at me around another mouthful of cake, swallowed, and then said, "Um, Jules." He reached across the counter. "You've got a little whipped cream… uh… "With a quick swipe of his finger, he snagged a fluffy dot that had somehow ended up on the end of my nose and then brushed it over my lips.

My tongue slipped out to catch it, but caught his finger instead. He lingered there on my lower lip, which trembled when he touched it. When he ran his finger over my mouth, heat flushed my cheeks. I blinked and sucked in a quick breath. "Will, I—"

"Shhh." He cupped my face and stroked my cheek with his thumb, tunneling his fingers under my hair. Tugging me closer, he leaned in and lightly touched his lips to mine.

When I didn't pull away, he increased the pressure, letting his tongue trace the seam between my lips. I put one hand up, ran it over his shoulder and around to the back of his neck, and opened my lips to him.

He stood and balanced himself with his other hand. For one second, I wondered why he didn't come around the island and take me in his arms, but I wasn't about to let go of the kiss to ask. His tongue met mine, and I tasted chocolate and sweet cream and

Will. A moan escaped into the kiss as he leaned in even more and the fire in my core increased. After a long delicious moment, I pulled away, slowly dropping back off my toes.

When I opened my eyes, he was staring at me. Heat flared in his expression, his pupils were pinpricks of emotion, and he swallowed hard.

My libido shouted at me to grab him and haul him to the closest bed. When I met his gaze, I knew in that moment all I had to do was give him a sign and he'd make love to me right then and there. Dear God, I wanted to, more than I'd ever wanted anything in my life, but I didn't say anything.

His breathing stuttered and his hands on my face shook. Then he surprised the hell out of me. He closed his eyes, and a deep breath later, tucked my tousled hair behind my ear and brushed his lips over mine.

"Good night, Slugger, thanks for dinner. It was great."

CHAPTER 9

I didn't realize I was holding my breath until the door closed quietly behind Will. I released it in a giant whoosh before I laid my forehead on the cool granite of the countertop.

Shit. Shit. Shit.

My heart still pounded, every nerve humming from that sensual contact. Good Lord, the boy could kiss. The *man* could kiss, because most certainly Will Brody was all man. I whimpered into the granite. This was not good. Not good at all. Raising my head, I cradled it in my palms and tried to gain some semblance of common sense.

Sex had reared its frustrating little head again, and I hadn't been so shocked about anything since the night Charlie dropped dead in my arms. Taking a deep breath, I poured some more wine into my glass and slugged it down. It never occurred to me that I'd desire anyone except my husband. I'd never wanted any man but Charlie, so when he died, I assumed I'd live my life as a widow and one day a grandmother, but never again as someone's lover. When was the appropriate time for a widow to start having carnal thoughts about another man? Only a year after her husband dies? And what would said husband think of me salivating over a man only a few years older than our son? Yeah, my life was changing and I was so much better, but was a fling with Will Brody the right path to take?

La Belle Femme had brought significance into my existence again, a way I could get out of my own head. I was having the time of my life assisting Sarah in putting together looks for those brave women. Who knew that my fashion sense would turn into a way to help others? I really believed it was my mission now, what would fulfill me. I could live happily by myself being a grandmother, a friend, and finding good causes. But Will Brody had thrown a monkey wrench into that line of thinking.

Did I need something more to feel fulfilled? Was *he* the something more?

Damn him anyway. Why did he have to be such a nice man? So kind and considerate and smart and talented? Okay, and he was damned good-looking, too. And why, oh why, did he have to tell me he was attracted to me? That particular declaration had stuck in my head like a frickin' earworm.

Maybe I should sleep with him and get it over with. Clearly, the heat between us wasn't going away. I could pretend that fire didn't exist, but when it flared like it did tonight, I had a hard time ignoring it. Maybe the sex would be terrible—hell, what did I know from good sex? The only person I'd ever been with was Charlie. We always had a very nice time in bed, at least as far as I was concerned, and he never complained.

But what if I slept with Will and the experience turned out...*bad*? What if we got naked and he was disgusted by my older body? I'd always taken good care of myself, but the effects of gravity after fifty-two years and the pale streaks on my belly from carrying babies were pretty evident—all the things Charlie had said he loved. Surely Will was used to younger, more toned, more experienced, sexier women. *Idiot!* Of course he was.

I finished the wine and tried to put him out of my mind. Eventually, I would have to deal with my attraction to Will—probably sooner than later—but tonight, *he'd* been the one to stop. He'd walked out after one kiss. Maybe I wasn't what he wanted anymore. Maybe it had occurred to him that he was kissing a woman who was way older than him and he'd lost his taste for cougar.

What a disheartening thought.

I smacked my forehead. What was I thinking! This game of emotional volleyball was wearing me out.

As I put the dishes in the dishwasher, my mind turned to Charlie. What *would* he think about Will? He'd always told me that if anything ever happened to him, I should go out and find some young stud and raise him up the way I wanted him. Charlie had been eight years older than me and already kind of set in his ways when we met. We joked all the time about me being his child bride. I'd done most of the adjusting in our marriage and was always happy for it to be that way. He'd raised me up the way he wanted me, no question about that. I became the perfect doctor's wife. He always said so.

"Ah, Charlie." I sighed and tossed the damp tea towels in the laundry room. "God, I miss you. I need your wisdom. I don't know what's right, but this guy is getting to me. Couldn't you just give me a little sign? Maybe a quick flash of lightning if it's okay for me to try Will Brody on for size." A glance around reassured me I was alone in the kitchen. Anyone who overheard me would be convinced I'd lost my mind, talking out loud to my dead husband. I peered out the window. No streak of lightning—the Chicago sky was dark except for the city lights reflected in Lake Michigan.

Thanks a bunch, Charlie. You are no help at all.

Grabbing my reading glasses from the bar, I wandered over to the computer and lifted the lid. The laptop hummed to life and Charlie's wallpaper appeared—a photo taken from the top of our beach steps, looking north up the shoreline of Lake Michigan toward Sleeping Bear Dune. A wave of homesickness washed over me. The view of the lake from my family room window was entirely different from Carrie and Liam's Chicago view. City lights gave an eerie yellow reflection to the water beyond, and I missed the blue-gray chop of the winter lake in Willow Bay.

Plopping in the chair, I clicked the browser, ready to check my email, then map out details of the fashion show so I'd have some hard facts for Sarah tomorrow. Money for a venue and a caterer was going to be the main issue, but I was hoping to get plenty of donations. Plus I figured I could convince Carrie to help me sell tickets. I'd considered a luncheon on a Sunday afternoon, maybe at a hotel. But a dinner dance would be fun too. My mind whirled as I scribbled a few notes and waited for webmail.

Will was right, having the email program set up for *my* account would be a ton easier than going through the Internet every time I wanted to check my messages. Maybe it was a simple thing to do. Idly, I clicked the email icon and watched the program open before me. Geesh, there *were* a lot of notes there for Charlie. I scrolled through them, mostly they were promotional things from wineries, gardening sites, and boating places. A marina in Traverse City had sent a message that the part he'd ordered for our pontoon was in. That arrived the day after Charlie died. I figured they'd restocked it, so I deleted it. The boat was in storage at Dixon's in Willow Bay. I had no idea when or if I'd ever use it again.

I continued scanning the list—eBay, Amazon, a company that sold parts for Jaguars, and a music store in San Francisco telling him that they were having their annual "Dollar Disc Days." I'd thought all this kind of thing went to his hospital email since he'd never once mentioned this other account. I touched Shift and deleted about thirty more junk emails before an address I didn't recognize appeared—*EJT135@sugartree.net*—with the simple subject, "Hey?" The message was dated three days after Charlie had died—the day before his funeral.

I double-clicked and it opened in a new window. My heart caught in my throat as I read the words:

Hey, Handsome,

Where've you been? I'm sorry I missed your call the other night. I was out with Peter and couldn't answer. But I slept with the phone under my pillow and your delicious message in my ear. I'm so hungry for you, so anxious to see you and touch you… just three more weeks and you'll be inside me…

E

I blinked twice, my mind still full of images of runways and dresses even as it occurred to me that something wasn't right. But I couldn't quite figure out *what* wasn't right, because it was like reading an email about how the sun didn't rise one morning. *Impossible.* So my mind went blank trying to figure out what this could possibly mean, since there was no way it could mean what it seemed to mean.

I scrolled down and found another one dated a few weeks earlier, but this time the subject was *RE: This Morning…* I opened it, my heart pounding in my ears.

I know, my lover. Mornings are my time to dream about you too, to remember your kisses, your hands on me. I lie in bed and wonder what you're doing at that very moment… probably a surgery or seeing patients, but I know I'm in the back of your mind. I loved talking to you while you drove home last night. One day, someone's going to stop at the overlook and you're going to have a hell of a time explaining what you're doing in the front seat of your Jag with your pants unzipped. But thinking of you touching yourself while I do the same here in my bed is incredibly erotic… June can't get here soon enough.

Missing you, Doc… and wanting you…

E

Below it was the note *E* was responding to.

Hey, Gorgeous,

I woke up this morning thinking about your beautiful breasts ... I miss their softness, letting my fingertips touch them ... I miss taking one of your nipples between my lips and gently sucking on it, and hearing you moan with pleasure ... Jesus, I miss hearing your sounds of pleasure ... I'm tempted to take my friend out right now, but I'll wait until tonight ... There's something very erotic about stroking myself to an orgasm and knowing that you're on the other end touching yourself, too...

Doc

His *friend?*

What the *hell?*

This couldn't possibly be my Charlie. Charlie Miles never once referred to his dick as his *friend.* I jokingly gave it a name when we first got married, and if we ever called it anything, it was Big Chuck. Heat rushed to my face and as I scrolled further, my fingers trembled. The emails were not frequent, maybe once every month or so, but the oldest message in the inbox, dated six months before Charlie died was again from *EJT135.*

My Doc,

Dear God, are you never going to arrive? I'm half-crazy with waiting, and longing to touch you again. Your plane should be landing in an hour and soon you'll be in my arms. I know it's not safe for us to text, but how I wish I could have a welcome text waiting on your phone for you when you land. Something titillating to make the drive up to me painfully erotic.

The wine is breathing and I'll be naked in bed... hurry, my lover...

E

Doc? Really? He hated being called *Doc.* Hell's bells, he damn near decked one of Kevin's poor buddies when he gave him a perfectly innocent "Hiya, Doc," one day on the beach steps.

That was at least ten years ago. There was no way on earth these messages were Charlie's.

Were they?

No! Charlie Miles was as faithful as the day was long. Perhaps he let some colleague borrow his email account for assignations with this *EJT* person. I tapped my fingernails on the edge of the table. My heart was in my throat. Panic was setting in.

Scrolling back to the top of the inbox, I scrutinized the list, trying to see if the note right after he died was indeed the last one. It was. There were newer emails, but no more from *EJT135*. They'd stopped arriving right after he died. Did that mean they *were* Charlie's? Unless… unless the other guy started collecting them somewhere else.

Dammit, I knew too little about how the Internet worked to know what was possible. I'd always just gotten my email from my email account. I'd used the same email address since the day we signed up all those years ago. I knew how to shop online and Google any topic, but the technical stuff was beyond me. I clutched my throat. Pain was building inside me, making clear thought more and more difficult.

A list to the left of the inbox indicated an archives folder.

Ah, okay, older emails.

I clicked it and got another inventory of folders, including another inbox. When I clicked, a list showed up. All the emails in the archive inbox folder were from *EJT135*—according to the counter, 227 of them dating back two years, which was about when Charlie bought the computer.

I read a few of them—they were all the same. Passionate, sexy, full of EJT's longing for Doc and Doc's reciprocal hunger.

Jesus Christ!

I slammed the lid on the laptop and paced the length of the apartment, then back again.

Not my Charlie. God, please.

This Doc had a Jag and he was a surgeon. Arms crossed over my belly, I stared out across the city lights to Lake Michigan, ransacking a list of Charlie's colleagues in my mind. Who else had a Jaguar? Who was most likely to be screwing around? *Frank Forrest?* He was always groping me at parties. And Jamie Talbot was a terrible flirt, frequently whispering wicked suggestions in my ear behind Charlie's back. But Frank drove a Hummer and Jamie, a BMW. Besides, both of them were smart enough to use their own private email accounts.

Whirling around, I stomped to the table and yanked the cover up again to read more of the messages. I couldn't seem to stop myself in spite of the knot forming in my stomach and the anguish clouding my mind. She adored him and he was nuts about her. Who was this woman? The relationship was long-distance. He had to fly to her and never once did they mention her coming to see him. An idea occurred to me—when was the last time Charlie went to a medical conference?

One of the tabs at the side of the program window was for a calendar. I found it and furiously clicked the arrow to go back to June year before last. *Oh, God!* He'd had a cardiology conference scheduled for that last week in June, but it didn't say where. Did I know about that?

Oh, wait, he saw her six months before he died... either August or September of last year.

Was he away then? My brain was so muddled, I couldn't remember. I went back to September, but there was nothing listed there.

Thank God.

I moved one month back and scanned the August calendar. Dear Lord in heaven, he'd had a conference at the end of August last year. Bile rose in my throat. *Where?* Crap, the location wasn't listed. He'd just put "conference" in a four-day time span. *What the hell?* Who doesn't list locations and times on their calendar?

Someone trying to hide something, apparently. But he never let anyone on this computer—why would he hide his itinerary? Possibly because there was no itinerary beyond falling into EJT's bed.

Where had he been last winter? Right before he died? Menopausal short-term memory loss meant I barely remembered what I ate for breakfast that morning, let alone where my busy husband had traveled over a year ago. I had to think.

I couldn't think. Stabbing pain pierced my heart, and suddenly my entire body ached and I doubled over with the agony of the discovery. It hurt so badly, I couldn't even cry and the fact that I remained dry-eyed confused and scared me. I'd never know this kind of heart hurt before. Not ever. This was worse than Charlie's death. Was there such a thing as pain so terrible you couldn't even cry?

Charlie'd had an affair.

For at least two years that I knew of for sure.

My mind was racing, but it was going nowhere as hurt and fear turned into hot anger that began to build in my brain.

The bastard!

I slammed the lid down on the computer again, kicked the chair back, and watched it clatter to the floor as a red veil of rage fell over my thoughts.

The rotten, cheating son of a bitch!

I grabbed my wine glass from the counter and hurled it into the sink, where it shattered into a hundred sparkling shards.

Oh, God, Carrie's crystal!

Somehow, I figured she'd forgive me given the circumstances. My stomach burned and my head pounded as I stormed through the apartment, trying desperately to find something to destroy.

When I got to the bedroom, I spotted the framed photograph of Charlie on the bedside table. Carrie had taken it a couple of years ago—he was drop-dead gorgeous in a yellow polo shirt, standing on our deck, laughing with Liam. His dark grey, leonine mane was swept back from his forehead, his white teeth straight and perfect, and his rugged features almost too handsome.

"You bastard," I whispered. And then I shouted, "Bastard! Fucker!" before yanking the photo from its mahogany frame. I ripped the picture in two and then ripped it again and again until it was nothing but confetti.

It didn't help.

Now too *angry* to cry, I hurled the frame across the room where it landed with unsatisfactory plop in the laundry basket by the bathroom door. I had to get out of there. I needed a drink, a walk, something… *someone* to help me make sense of this horrifying discovery.

Suddenly, I knew exactly where to go, exactly who to see. Snatching my keys from the dresser, I shoved them my pocket and headed out the door.

CHAPTER 10

I jammed my finger hard on the doorbell, at the same time glancing up at the clock above the elevators—midnight was only minutes away. Will was probably closing up shop for the night. What would he think when he peeked through the peephole and saw me standing outside in the hallway, barefoot and tousled, red-faced and agitated? The door lock clicked.

"Julie? Everything okay?" Will's deep voice was laced with concern.

I simply gazed at him for a moment. His brow was furrowed, his eyes dark blue in the dim hallway lighting. Then I reached for him, gripping his shirt front in one hand and tugging him toward me. My other hand snaked around his neck as I brought his lips down to mine in a searing kiss right there in the doorway.

I didn't give him any time to react. Instead, I pushed him back into his apartment and shoved the door closed behind me. All the while my mouth was pressed to his. Instinct must've kicked in because he responded in kind, opening my lips with an eager tongue. He still tasted of wine and chocolate, and the delicious scent of him filled my nostrils as we shared deep hungry kisses. He let his hands wander at will, up and down my spine and down over my hips, and I felt him rise to attention, already hard against my belly.

Jerking his shirt out of his pants, I found the skin of his back, and my fingers drew sensual circles there, right above his belt. He didn't fight me or stop to question what had happened or why I was there. No, he simply slid one hand down my butt to my thighs and lifted me into his arms. I rained tiny kisses down his cheek to his neck as I nuzzled there. My tongue tasted the skin beneath the neckline of his shirt, making goose pimples rise wherever I touched.

Amazingly, he got to the bedroom without bumping into anything and lowered me to his bed. Pulling back, his gaze locked on mine.

Before he could speak, I put my finger to his lips. "Shh…" My voice cracked. "Please…"

He pushed my finger away, nodding as he lowered his head.

Will's lips on mine sent heat straight to my center, adding even more fuel to the bonfire of rage that burned deep inside me.

Fuck you, Charlie. You're not the only one who can screw around.

I shoved that thought aside and concentrated on divesting Will of his shirt, yanking at the hem. He tugged it off, then pulled my sweater up and over my head. The urgency was contagious as we tossed our clothing away from us.

He ran one finger over my collarbone and down between my breasts, stopping at the center clip of my bra. His lips followed, touching my skin, his tongue tracing a line over each breast. The hair on his chest tickled my palms as I slid them over his broad muscles, wondering idly if he worked out in the gym downstairs. There wasn't an ounce of excess flesh on the man—unlike Charlie, the old bastard, whose body had begun to go soft with age before he died. I'd even teased him a little last time we'd showered together.

Focus, Julie! You have a deliciously handsome man unhooking your bra, for God's sake, and besides… Charlie's dead.

Will cupped my breast, molding and caressing. A quick intake of breath and his lips closed over my nipple. Dear God, I'd forgotten the unrelenting pleasure of a man's mouth on me, and Will Brody was already demonstrating he was truly gifted. His tongue swirled around my erect nipple, sending a spasm of sensation to my core. I ran my fingers over his scalp, amazed to feel only his thick, spiky hair.

Huh, barely any product.

Another inane thought, dumbass. Just concentrate.

I did, closing my eyes and letting my head fall back on his pillows. He moved his mouth lower to the flesh under my breast before kissing his way down my belly. I reached between us to unzip my jeans, but he stopped me.

"Let me." His voice was husky and when he raised his head, his eyes were dark with passion.

My heart sped up at his expression, so full of wonder and something else… some other emotion I recognized but couldn't define. Suddenly, I wanted this man. I wanted him so badly I could taste it. I pulled him up to kiss him again, ravaging his mouth as hunger built in me. A dam had burst, and the wall I'd erected in the months since Charlie's death fell. Desire crashed over me. I *needed* Will's touch, his pure unadulterated admiration of me, more than I'd ever needed anything in my life.

He was trying to be gentle, his hands sliding slowly into the waist of my jeans and easing them down as we explored one another, but I didn't want gentle. I pushed his hands aside and shoved my jeans and panties down, kicking them away even as I groped for the snap on his pants. When the back of my hand brushed over his erection, he caught his breath. I reached for him, encircling his hardness with my fingers as he squirmed out of the rest of his clothes.

I stroked and tugged while his hand slipped down my belly to find the sensitive place between my legs—a place I'd forgotten even existed. It had been so long since I'd been touched, for a moment, I worried that my body wouldn't remember how to respond. But I was there, I was engaged, raising my hips off the bed to Will's exploring fingers. He created magic there, sending spasms of pleasure through me.

His breath was hot on my throat and on my collarbone where he pressed his lips to my skin before he again found my nipples. First one, then the other, sucking and licking, creating mindless heat deep inside me—heat like I'd never known before. One finger slid into me, then a second, while his thumb rubbed and massaged.

"*Now*, Will," I whispered, opening my legs. "Please… "

Drawing back, he fumbled in the bedside drawer and for a second, I didn't realize what he was doing.

Condom. Oh yes, of course.

Before I could give the matter another moment's thought, he was sheathed and filling me up.

Dear God in heaven, I forgot. I forgot how delicious a man inside me feels.

He pulled back slowly and then plunged into me before pulling back oh-so-slowly again. I moaned and slid my hands down his brawny back to his butt, pressing my fingers into his muscled flesh, urging him on. All I wanted was for him to take me, to ease the ache.

We moved together in a perfect familiar rhythm, and I slipped further into the moment, unable to think of anything except Will, right now, inside me. My hips rose to meet his as he thrust deeper into me, so deep he found the emptiness in my soul and filled up the places I thought would never be filled again. Overwhelmed at the erotic power of his touch, I spiraled into mindlessness, crying out as I fell over the edge into oblivion.

Will hurried into the bathroom, which gave me a chance to pull the sheet up over my nakedness. I couldn't believe what I'd just done.

Oh, God. Oh, God.

Holy shit. I'd just used a wonderful, kind man to exact sexual revenge on my dead husband. That had to be six kinds of sick. But damn, Will Brody sure knew his way around a woman's body. I blushed, thinking of how I'd reacted to his touch, moaning and crying out, and dear lord, did I scream? Oh surely not. Did I?

When he came back out, I gave him a wan smile and blurted, "I never make noise when I have sex, Will."

He grinned. "Um… yes, you do."

"I mean, I *usually* don't make noise." Heat flushed my cheeks. God, he was gorgeous, all tousled and looking tasty enough to eat.

"I'm going to attribute that to mastery of the art, okay?" Giving me a wink, he slipped into bed and scooped me into his arms. "Next time, we'll go slow, and I'll see if I can make you meow."

"Next time?" I hoped he realized I wasn't being coy. My eyes welled up with tears. "Will, I—"

"No," he said, brushing my hair back off my face. "Shh… we're good. *This* is good. No overthinking, okay?"

"I need to tell you why…" My voice quavered as I sniffed.

With one finger, he stroked the rivulet of tears from my cheek. "Only if you want to. You don't have to talk about it. I'm just glad you came… and I mean that on several different levels."

The giggle he was going for emerged and I turned to him, kissing his chest, wetting his skin with my tears even as I shook with laughter. He lifted my chin and pressed his lips to mine. I tasted my salty tears and wine and still the faintest hint of chocolate. My tongue sought his and set off reactions in his lower body that surprised the hell out of me—Charlie had never been back on deck that quickly before. He showed me his need by cupping my behind and pressing me firmly against his erection.

His kisses left me breathless and incredulous. I was naked with another man. I was in his bed, cuddled up next to him, my hands wandering over his chest and sliding down to his hip. His hand slipped between my thighs, and he tugged my leg over his hip, pushing his hard-on against the wet heat between my legs.

I moved up, adjusting my position as we kissed deep hungry kisses. I pushed him over onto his back and straddled him.

But he caught me before I impaled myself on him. "Wait," he gasped. "Condom." He could barely get the word out. "Oh, crap… "

"What?" The word came out on a husky breath while I kissed down his chin and neck.

His grip on my hips tightened and he tipped his head back on the pillow. "Um… I… I'm all out." He tugged my head up so he could he look into my eyes. "Earlier… that was my last one."

"Will, it's too late in my life for birth control." I leaned back down to let my tongue glide over his nipple again and then suck it as he'd done to mine earlier. He drew a ragged breath. I'd never realized a man's nipples could be so sensitive. "Is there anything *you* need to tell *me* about?"

"Not a thing." He arched his back, nestling into the cleft between my legs and moving up and down, but not entering me.

"Good, me, either—" On those words, I sat up, sliding back until I was perched on his thighs. "Oh, God, at… at least I don't think so." I closed my eyes and slipped off him onto the bed, as my stomach clenched. Oh, hell! If Charlie had slept around, maybe I was carrying around all kinds of vermin. "Shit!" I yanked the sheet back up to cover myself.

He rolled over. "What just happened?" With one finger, he turned my face toward him, but I resisted.

"That *bastard!*" I hit the mattress with one fist. "That goddamned son of a bitch. He cheated on me, Will. God knows how many women he was with. Hell's bells, I could be crawling with STDs and not even know it." Sitting up, I threw off the covers. "I need a shower. I gotta get tested."

"Whoa, hang on." He reached for me, but missed as I hopped off the bed.

I ran into the bathroom with Will hot on my heels. The harsh light damn near blinded me when I flipped the switch.

Will blinked too, squinting at me. "Julie, slow down. Talk to me."

Grabbing a clean washcloth from the rack by the shower, I twisted the knob. Water rushed from the double shower heads, soaking us as we stood by the open glass door. Tears burned in my eyes and my lower lip trembled before I caught it between my teeth.

All of a sudden, I let out a wail that would've woke the neighbors if Will hadn't had his walls soundproofed for guitar playing. I bent over, arms crossed over my belly, and sobbed. I couldn't even speak. I couldn't find words to tell him how I'd gone into Charlie's old email box and found those notes from his lover. Pain cut through me so sharply I couldn't stop crying long enough to admit what had brought me to his bed.

He reached down to lift my face to his. It was right there in his eyes. He'd figured it out. Will knew exactly why I'd knocked on his door and why I'd jumped him after pretending for so long that I wasn't in the slightest interested. Now, he'd shove me away and probably never speak to me again. I'd used him. It was wrong, so very wrong. He gazed into my eyes, his own expression unreadable at first. But instead of fury, his face softened with sympathy.

"Oh, baby… I'm so sorry," he whispered.

Then he guided me into the steamy shower, closed the door, and wrapped his arms around me, rocking with me under the warm spray while I wept.

CHAPTER 11

"No. I don't want you to fix it. Just get rid of it, okay?"
Less than twenty-four hours after I'd had the worst news and the best sex of my life, Will and I were arguing. "Throw it off the balcony. Toss it in the lake. Put it in the street and let the damn garbage truck run it over. Get it out of my sight. Please?"

"Julie, that's dumb." Will fidgeted with the mouse next to Charlie's laptop. "A waste of a perfectly good and very expensive laptop. How about if I remove the email program and reinstall a brand new one?" His voice took on a coaxing tone which at that moment was irritating the hell out of me.

"*No.*"

I wanted the fucking thing out of the apartment and out of my life. I never wanted to see it again.

"You're acting like a child." Pulling the little optical thingy from the side of the computer, he fitted it into the bottom of the mouse.

"You should know." A catty thing to say, but he was missing the point entirely. And I knew for a fact he wasn't that obtuse. Couldn't he see that the laptop represented more than Charlie's infidelity? That it mocked the last thirty years of my existence?

"Jules, it's not the computer's fault." He'd let my snarky retort go.

He was way too nice a guy—he only wanted to help me deal with the devastating discovery of Charlie's affair. Or *affairs*—who the hell knew? I was still so angry I could barely breathe, and dammit, the son of a bitch wasn't around to scream at… or kick in the balls. At that moment, I could've knocked Charlie's lights out if he'd been present.

"I know that." I paced the high-ceilinged kitchen in Carrie's apartment, debating the wisdom of trying to explain my attitude to Will. How could I make him understand? "It's that he used that laptop to talk to *her,* to be with *her.*" I swallowed hard, determined not to cry again. He'd certainly had enough of my tears last night.

"So now… what? It has cooties?"

I couldn't help it, I burst out laughing. I hadn't heard that word since I was twelve. He was right, of course, but I simply couldn't bear the thought of ever touching the machine again. I held one hand out. "Tell you what, I'll keep the mouse, it's mine. The rest of it goes. Now, please."

"How about I wipe the hard drive?" he offered. "Reload the programs and start fresh and clean."

I paused, staring at the laptop. Just the sight of it left a bitter taste in my mouth, but curiosity niggled in the back of my mind. If I was ever going to know the whole story, I might need the computer and the emails to figure out who she was. Did I want to know? My head shouted, *yes, find her and kick her butt,* but my heart cringed at the very thought.

Before I could say anything, Will leaned over to grab the leather bag under the table. "The bag, too?"

"Everything."

"Do you want to check it and make sure there's nothing in it you want to keep?"

"Like what?"

"I don't know. Papers? Mail? Cash? Stuff you might need?" Holding the bag up, he shook it.

"Oh, for the love of—" For the life of me, I didn't want to touch Charlie's laptop satchel. Frankly, it didn't matter what was in it.

Will stared at me, one brow raised, daring me to take it from his fingers.

I reached for it, jerked the zipper on the front pouch, and emptied it onto the countertop. A roll of butter rum Lifesavers hit the granite, along with three pens, a flash drive, and a handful of change. In the slim side pocket was one of Charlie's ten or twelve pairs of reading glasses—the rimless ones he'd told me he'd lost.

Another lie. The bastard.

The cords for recharging the computer fell out of the main compartment and the larger pocket on the back held a *New Yorker* magazine, a brochure from Tuckaway Winery, six wine corks— also from Tuckaway—and two unused Band-Aids.

I tossed the bag and the cords to Will. "No secret documents. No condoms. No tell-all journal." I'd given up trying to keep the anger out of my tone.

"You're sure?" He stuffed the computer in the bag and zipped it up as I swept the rest of the stuff off the counter into the trash compactor.

"Yes."

"Julie, listen." Tucking one finger under my chin, Will lifted my face to his. "At some point, you gotta deal with this."

Twisting away, I turned to stare out the breakfast nook window at the lake in the distance, my hands curled into fists at my sides. Will put his arm around me and tugged me back against him. I let my head rest against his strong chest.

Deal with it.

Yep, that *was* what I needed to do. "I can't, Will." Voice quivering, I gulped back tears. "It hurts. Dear God, it hurts and now I'm such a mess again."

"Julie, come on—" His hand smoothed down my back, easing the tension in my spine. "You've had some bad news and—"

I jammed my elbow into his stomach, pushing him away from me. "Bad news?" My voice rose to shrill on the words. "Seriously? That's what you call it? I find out my perfect marriage was a nothing but a–a sham and you call that *bad news?* Jesus, Will. You have no idea what I'm feeling, do you? Can you even imagine what it's like to find out the man you thought adored you was busy doing it with another woman while you were taking care of his house, his kids… his *life?*"

A torrent of words poured out of me as Will stood still as a statue. I couldn't stop them. "The bastard was screwing around with God knows how many women the whole time he was pretending to be this perfect husband and father. Oh, and don't forget—*Dr. Wonderful.* Everyone in that damn town believed he was right next door to a saint." I took a breath before continuing to seethe. "Oh yeah, Saint Charlie… works the soup kitchen in Traverse City every Thanksgiving morning, spends hours sitting with patients post-surgery, attends PTA events—even if it means he has to come in late because of an emergency—never misses a single goddamned anniversary or birthday. Not once."

I snorted. "Don't think I didn't wear *that* like a badge of honor when my friends bitched about their husbands forgetting special days. Hell, Charlie brought me flowers or jewelry or something on the anniversary of the day we met, for sweet Christ's sake."

"Julie, take a breath. Come here." Will crossed to me and laid his hands on my shoulders. "If you need to rant, then rant. But let me help you."

"*How?* How can you help me?" Squirming out of his grasp, I paced the kitchen into the dining room, the living room, casting about desperately for something I could throw. Rage boiled inside me. "I just want to hit something, break something. To hurt someone. I've never been this angry in my life."

"Here." He met me by the grand piano and handed me… *his shoe?*

I gazed up at him. "What?"

"Throw it. Hurl it against the door. If it leaves a mark, we'll get it fixed."

"It's okay." I managed a weak smile. "Thanks, but I don't need to throw your shoe."

"Do it," he encouraged, his head cocked toward the wood front door. "Just chuck it. You'll feel better, I promise." Obviously he sensed my hesitation because he toed off his other loafer. "Look. Over there. Isn't that Charlie by the door? Let him have it."

I hefted the shoe before I drew back and launched it with every ounce of strength I could muster.

Take that, you asshat.

The leather loafer hit the door with a very satisfactory whump.

"You got him. Right on his big fat head." Will tossed me his other shoe. "Do it again. I think he's still conscious."

His grin was infectious. So with a wicked smile, I took a pitcher's stance, wound up, and threw the loafer as hard as I could.

"And he's out!" Will shouted with a raucous hoot. "Want to do it again? Take your shoes off."

But I was exhausted and suddenly out of the mood to lob any more shoe grenades. "Thanks, Will." My voice cracked.

No, goddammit, no more tears! I refuse to cry over that man, ever again.

Instead, I brushed past him to the kitchen where I opened the wine fridge. "I'm thinking a big glass of wine would be good about now."

"It's five o'clock somewhere." Will agreed and took the bottle of wine from me. "Go sit on the couch. I'll bring it to you."

I flopped on the sofa as he found the corkscrew and opened the pinot noir I'd pulled from Liam and Carrie's stash. After filling two glasses, he joined me. I could tell he was trying unobtrusively to judge my frame of mind. I stared off into space as I sipped, shoving the hurt down.

I wanted to explain the mishmash of emotions roiling inside me. *Betrayed?* Most certainly. *Hurt?* Beyond words. *Furious?* Absolutely. But as I sat there, I went from angry to sad to confused, and it must have shown on my face.

"Talk to me," he coaxed. "What're you thinking?"

"Who is she?" In one rather ungraceful move, I sat up, curled my feet under me, and faced him.

He shrugged and took a drink of wine. "Who knows?"

"No. Really. Who *is* she?"

Teeth worrying my lower lip, I stared at him, but I wasn't really seeing him. Instead, I was racking my mind, sorting through over thirty years' worth of friendships, acquaintances, work colleagues—anyone at all Charlie might have been screwing.

"Why do you need to know who she is? Who any of them were?" He slid over and tugged me into his arms without spilling a drop of wine from either of our glasses. "He's gone. It's over."

I settled against his broad chest, drawing comfort from the warmth of his body next to mine. "But... I think... I think he *loved* her. I read the emails. They were crazy about each other." A long sip of wine and several deep sighs later, I went on, relentless in my examination. "I don't know how many women there were over the years, but *this* one wasn't a one-night stand, Will. Or even a fling. They were involved for at least two years that I know of. It could've been longer than that."

"Again, why do you need to know anything else?" Tipping his

head to one side, he peered into my eyes. Gently, he brushed my hair back from my face. "How will it help you to know this one's name?"

"I don't know." With a shrug, I cuddled closer to him, wishing like crazy that he could simply erase all this from my mind.

"Say you find out. Will it stop there?" The question was reasonable, and when I stared up at him, he continued. "Then will you have to go on a hunt for every floozy he ever hooked up with?"

"I don't know."

"Let it go." Easing my now-empty wine glass from my fingers, he set both our glasses on the table before he wrapped his arms around me. "Just let it go." His fingers sifted through my hair while his other hand smoothed the tense muscles of my back.

I relaxed against him. I realized now that, although I'd gotten so much better since being in Chicago, I was still fragile. News of Charlie's double life had devastated me. I hadn't slept at all after I left Will's place. Confused and too sick and angry to lie still, I'd paced the apartment the rest of the night, going from one room to another, staring out at the city lights, rehashing my marriage in my head. How could I have been so blind? How did I not see it? And who was she? What was her hold on my husband?

I knew there had to be a way to figure out who the woman was—maybe do a reverse search on the email address? Was that even possible? Will would help me if asked him to. If I could find this one, maybe she'd lead me to the others—if there were others. Oh hell, there *had* to be others. A cheater never cheated just one time, did he? Maybe I didn't want to know how many other women there'd been. Perhaps simply finding out who Charlie had been screwing around with at the end would give me some sort of peace.

Sliding my arm across his stomach, I allowed myself to settle deeper into Will's embrace, even though I wasn't entirely comfortable with the new turn in our relationship. Ironic because *I* was the one who'd taken it to a higher level. When I'd left him last night, I had no idea where we were headed or if I even wanted it to go anywhere, but I'd stopped fighting the attraction.

The moment he appeared at my door with breakfast and a concerned smile, it was obvious he was all in. He wanted me despite how I'd used him, despite the difference in our ages, and despite the fact that I was an emotional basket case. He was sticking. I had to decide if I was.

But not now. Not today.

We turned together and stretched out on the sofa. Will held me close, and his breathing grew slower and more rhythmic. I curled into his warm body and shut my eyes too.

CHAPTER 12

Norah Jones woke me with a start. Dopey from sleep, I raised my head from Will's warm chest, blinking to clear my contacts.

Where the hell's my phone?

The ringing stopped then started up again as I pulled myself off the couch—off Will—and stumbled into the kitchen to retrieve it from the counter.

"Mom?" Urgency colored Kevin's voice. "Hey, Mom?"

"I'm here, honey. What's up?" I rubbed my face, before peering at the clock on the microwave. Two-thirty in the afternoon. God, I'd really gone down for the count. We'd curled up together around noon or so.

Will wandered in from the living room, yawning and stretching like a cat. With his sweatshirt pulled up and his t-shirt hanging out of his khakis, he looked rumpled and sexy. As he raised his arms above his head, I got a peek of tanned stomach that sent a tingle right through me.

"Meg's in labor." Urgency shifted into excitement in Kevin's tone. "We're timing contractions. They're nine minutes apart."

"Kevin, she's early." I tried to remember what they'd told me a few weeks ago about the dates being mixed up. "Isn't it too soon? I thought she wasn't due for three more weeks."

"Apparently, the baby's decided to come now. Her water broke a couple of hours ago."

"Are you at the birthing center?" My heart pounded. I was about to become a *grandmother.*

"Yup. We came right after. The OB says it'll be sometime in the next eighteen hours." Kevin's breathing came fast, as if he'd been running. "Mom, we're having a baby."

"You sure are, honey." I gave Will a giant smile as he pulled open the fridge and perused its contents. "Meg's in labor," I whispered.

His eyebrows shot up. "Is it going to happen today?" After grabbing two bottles of water, he bumped the door shut with his elbow.

"I think so." With a finger in the air to hold Will's questions, I focused on Kevin, who was also chattering to Meg in the background. "Kev, tell Meg I'm on the way, okay?"

I had to get to San Francisco. Meg's parents had died when she was a teenager. Her older sister, Sherry, raised her until she went to college at Michigan State, where she met my son. She had no other close family, and I'd promised to be there for the birth of the first child of this new generation. "Where's Sherry?"

"In Denmark at a physics conference. I left her a message and texted twice. No answer yet. She'll be wrecked if she misses this, but I don't know what else to do." Kevin's unerring sense of hyper-responsibility for everyone had already kicked in. "Mom, call the airline and talk to them in person. You'll get a better fare. Tell them you're coming for the birth of your first grandchild... Oh, my God! You're going to be a grandma." He chuckled and I heard Meg giggling, too. "Are you ready for that?"

"More than you know." In my mind, I was already packing and figuring out the logistics of getting from the airport in San

Francisco to the kids' apartment in the city. Which BART station was closest to their place? Was it Powell?

Taking a deep breath, I focused. "I'm going to go now and get things together. I'll call you back when I know what flight I'm taking."

"Okay, I'll come get you at the airport."

"Absolutely not," I insisted. "I'll BART to you and call you when I get off the train."

"Mom… "Worry seeped into his voice.

"Kevin… "I parroted his doubtful tone. "Stay with your wife. I'll be there soon."

"I love you, Mom. Hurry."

"I love you, too. Give Meg a hug and tell her I'm on my way. I'll see you soon." I stuck the phone in my pocket and twirled around once before throwing my arms around Will's neck.

Engulfing me in a giant hug, he kissed me soundly. "A baby," he said when he released the kiss and tipped his head down to stare into my eyes. "You're gonna be the hottest grandma in the world."

I rested my forehead against his shoulder for a moment. "You dope. God, I can hardly believe it." When I glanced up at him, his expression was full of wonder and so much affection I didn't even try to resist kissing him again. I pressed my mouth to his, letting my tongue run along his lower lip, seeking entry.

I'll give you hot grandma, baby.

Hands sliding down my spine to my hips, he pulled me hard against him, opening the kiss even more, tangling his tongue with mine. His arousal pressed against my belly as his tongue teased. How amazing, the effect our kisses had on him… and on me. Immediately, I wanted to ransack Carrie and Liam's apartment for a condom and haul him back to my bed. Dear God in heaven, the man's kisses sent me right to mindlessness. I pressed closer as his hands sought my behind.

Dammit.

At that moment, I needed to be thinking and planning, not falling into ecstasy with Will. With great reluctance, I broke the embrace.

"I have to call the airline and book a flight," I said, rubbing my lips as if I could keep the imprint of his mouth there. "And I have to pack and close up... oh, and call Sarah at the shop... and Carrie... and get a shower... "

"You call Sarah. I'll get you a flight." He pulled out his cell phone and touched the screen. "Do you need a hotel or will you stay with the kids?"

"A hotel, definitely. There's a little boutique hotel just a couple of blocks from them where Char—where I've stayed before," I amended quickly, and a stab of pain hit me in the gut at the very thought of my dead husband.

Not now. More important things to worry about.

With a shake of my head, I scooted toward the bedroom. "I'll find the number and call. The kids don't need me staying in that tiny apartment with them."

Will stopped. "Hey?"

When I turned, the expression on his face—like a kid who thought he might be in trouble—puzzled me.

"Do you... do you want me to come with you?" he asked.

I gazed at him for a moment, wishing like anything I could say *yes, yes, come with me.* But that would be a mistake. I had to do this on my own, plus I couldn't face any questions from the kids about why Liam's manager was traveling with me. Instead, I teased. "You just want to see me turn into a granny."

With a grin, he was beside me in four long strides. "A very sexy granny... a delectable, delicious... "The words got lost as his lips found mine.

Enticing as it was to stay in Will's arms, to kiss him until our lips were too swollen to speak, I had to get going. After a few seconds, I pulled away. "Will, I've *got* to get busy."

"Finding you a flight, right now." He released me to display his phone, already on the airline's website. "Got the number. I'm calling. Go shower." A pat on my behind sent me down the hall.

"Try the old *this is an emergency* tactic. Maybe they'll find a seat for me in first class," I called over my shoulder.

The queue at airport security was long, and Will insisted on staying with me while I waited and fidgeted. I'd only packed a small bag that I was carrying on, so we'd avoided the ticket counters altogether, thank God. The line there was even longer. He'd scored with the airline. I had a first-class seat on a non-stop flight that left at five-thirty and landed at SFO at about eight in the evening. He'd hustled me into a cab and I made my hotel reservations on the ride to O'Hare.

Dropping me at the Departures door wasn't even an option for Will, even though I'd argued with him as he paid the driver. Secretly, I was glad. I wanted as much time with him as I could get, even if it meant we spent it standing in the airport security line.

"No BART at night, Julie," he said, watching me dig my driver's license out of my overstuffed wallet. The boarding pass I had clenched between my lips kept me from arguing, so he reiterated while he had the opportunity. "I mean it. Take a cab. With your roll-on, that computer bag, and your purse, you'll be a damn target."

"Ah ha." I found the necessary ID and dropped the wallet back into my purse. "Oh, come on, I've ridden the BART plenty of times and besides—"

"Come on." Will's expression was full of worry. "Just take a cab, okay? Do it for me… and Kevin. He doesn't need to be worrying about you. What made you decide to bring this thing with you?" He took the computer bag from me as I tried to get organized for the TSA. "This morning, you were begging me to toss it in the dumpster."

"Okay, okay. I'll get a taxi." I bent down to untie my sneakers, steadying myself with a hand on his arm. "And I decided you were right. It *is* stupid to throw it out. It's an expensive laptop. And I want to be able to send Ryan and Renee pictures of their new nephew."

I hated being cagey with him, but I wasn't going to go into how I intended to figure out who Charlie's paramour was. He might've tried to talk me out of it.

A plan was already brewing in the back of my mind. I intended to figure out who the woman was, and I could use his laptop to do it. Now that the initial fury had settled down, I was curious—who the hell could be so enticing that he'd cheat on *me*, the woman he'd trained so well to adore and serve him?

"You're almost up, Jules." Will's voice brought me back to the airport.

I accepted the leather computer tote, tucked my shoes under my arm, and adjusted my shoulder bag, then reached one arm around his neck and gave him a hug. "Thanks. Thanks so much. For everything."

He pulled me close. He wasn't going to let me get away with a simple hug—a goodbye I'd give to one of my sons.

"I'm here, okay? All you gotta do is call." He gazed into my eyes, clearly trying hard to get a message across without making a declaration in front of the whole crowd.

When he touched his lips to my mouth, I melted. He increased the pressure, branding me with a kiss that would leave no doubt in anyone's mind—particularly mine—what our relationship might be.

"No overthinking us, Slugger," he whispered when he released me.

Weak in the knees, I simply stared at him. "Will... I... "

"No." He touched one finger to the tip of my nose. "Travel safe. Let me know you got there."

I swallowed hard and nodded before dragging the roll-on behind me as the line moved forward. At the metal detectors, I piled my belongings on the belt and glanced back one last time.

Will was still standing right where I'd left him. He shook his head and mouthed, "No overthinking."

With a tremulous smile and a flutter of my fingers, I nodded, then blew him a kiss.

CHAPTER 13

The moment was bound to come, and indeed it did as Kevin, Meg, and I sat in the room at the birthing center, admiring my new grandson. I'd managed to avoid any mention of Charlie since I'd arrived, but his name finally came up. And in a way that I would've called *foul* on except that my innocent son and his sweet wife had no idea that his father was a lying, cheating snake. Plus, they'd just become a real family—a fact that was beyond important to Kevin. It was all he'd wanted from the time he and Meg had said, "I do."

When I dropped my bags in the corner of the birthing room, Meg was nearly ready to deliver. After a quick hug for Kevin, I hurried to the other side of the bed and helped coach her through the last minutes of labor. Witnessing my grandson come into the world was an exhilarating experience. With quite a thatch of dark hair and my blue eyes, he was, well, *perfect*—almost a duplicate of his father as a newborn.

Kevin and an exhausted Meg watched as I cuddled and rocked him, their expressions tender enough to bring tears to my eyes. "Okay," I said, touching the baby's tiny nose with my fingertip. "So what's this little guy's name?"

Rising from his seat on the bed next to Meg, my son came over to kneel by the rocking chair. "Meg and I agreed, Mom. We're naming him after Dad." Kevin's eyes filled as he said the name I'd been avoiding. "Charles Edward Miles. the Second."

My heart sank, and I dropped my gaze back to the baby, fearful that my disappointment might show. I knew they'd chosen the name to please me because Kevin believed it would make me happy to honor his dad. They didn't know about Charlie's deception or that he was anything but the perfect father and husband.

I took a deep breath that could have been interpreted in any way, even happiness. No way was I going to spoil this moment for them. Gulping, I cupped Kevin's cheek. "That's wonderful. What shall we call him?"

Kevin's smile was worth the effort of concealing my own heartache. "We thought maybe *Eddie*. That way he'll have his own name, even though we named him after Dad." He leaned forward to press a quick kiss on my cheek. "What do you think?"

"I love it." Gazing down at the sleeping infant, I touched my lips to his forehead, and the cotton cap they'd put on him after delivery tickled my nose. Biting my lip, I vowed silently that I wouldn't allow this precious child to be a constant reminder of Charlie's infidelity, even if he was his namesake.

Eddie.

I could work with that.

A round midnight, when Meg and the baby were settled in the room at the birthing center, Kevin and I stopped for a beer and a sandwich at a pub near the hotel. Sitting in the dim bar, we faced each other across the booth, both too tired to even attempt conversation. As I gazed at him, his resemblance to his father hit me full force. I hadn't seen him since he'd flown by home on business right before Thanksgiving. Stubble shadowed his cheeks, his hair was awry, and his eyes were smudged with weariness but still shining. He was Charlie, but he was the impassioned, young Charlie who'd vowed eternal devotion to me, not that other guy—the one who'd made a mockery of my life.

"Whew." He smiled at me wanly. "I'm completely jacked, but I'm too tired to show it."

"I can imagine." Reaching across the table, I took his hand. "I remember how exhausted we were when you were born."

"He's beautiful, isn't he?"

"He's gorgeous, Kev." I gave his fingers a squeeze as the waiter set our beers in front of us. "To Eddie. Welcome to the world." I raised my glass.

"Thanks for coming out, Mom." Kevin swiped foam off his lip with his napkin. "We couldn't have done it without you."

"Oh, I'm fairly sure he would have made his appearance whether I was here or not." I took another sip of icy beer. "Once they decide they're ready to come out, it's pretty hard to stop them."

"I wish Dad were here."

"I know you do." I gave him a small smile.

"He'd have been so into this, you know?" Kevin's wistful expression nearly crushed my heart. "Remember how he broke out the expensive champagne when we told you guys we were trying to get pregnant?"

I nodded. Charlie would've been excited about becoming a grandfather. He'd talked about babies constantly after Kevin and Meg told us they were going to start a family. Odd that he'd even given it a moment's thought, considering the double life he'd been leading. Blood pounded in my ears, so I took a long drink of beer and temporarily willed away the anger. I was going to have to deal with this. I couldn't keep getting furious every time the man's name was mentioned. That simply wasn't going to work, particularly around my kids.

Our kids.

We drank in tired silence for a few minutes until our food arrived. Kevin dove into his cheeseburger with gusto, and I was surprised at how hungry I was. The chicken sandwich tasted delicious, and the pub made killer fries.

Kevin leaned back in the booth, crossing his arms over his chest. It was a Charlie posture—I'd seen it hundreds of times when he was preparing to say something he considered important. The resemblances between my dead husband and my older son seemed so much more evident at that moment. I mused on the reasons for this phenomenon as Kevin spoke.

"Mom, you look great." He eyed me as I wolfed down the last of my fries. "Damn good, in fact. How are things going? I mean… *really*?"

"I *am* good, honey." I dabbed at my lips with my napkin. "Really," I added when he raised one brow. "I'm busy in Chicago, volunteering at a boutique that's associated with a women's shelter. I love the work, and it's a great cause. I'm having fun, and it keeps my mind occupied. I'm swimming in the pool at the apartment building, and I'm getting stronger every day. I'm seeing the therapist once a week and she's already halved my antidepressants," I enumerated, determined to keep a smile on my face.

"I ran into Liam in Washington last month. I was there on business, and he was conducting the National Philharmonic at the music center at Strathmore."

"Did you get to go? How was it?"

"Yeah, he left me a ticket at will-call." Kevin popped a couple of fries into his mouth. "It was great, but afterward, we had a drink and talked about… well, about *you*."

"Ah, so that's why my ears were burning a few weeks ago." A weak attempt at humor on my part, which Kevin ignored.

"He and Carrie think you're better in Chicago—away from home. How long will you stay there do you think?"

I shrugged. "Right now, it's one day at a time."

"Well, Liam thinks you should stay as long as you want to."

"I'll see. I know I'd miss the lake in the summer."

Where was the kid heading? I didn't have to wait past his next words to find out.

"Mom, your house is so big. Maybe you should think about putting it on the market. I know real estate's slow right now, but things always pick up around there in the spring. I hate the idea of you rattling around there all by yourself." He said it fast, in one breath as he fidgeted with his fries and avoided my gaze.

If I'd been being perfectly honest with him at that moment, I would've told him I never wanted to go near Charlie Miles's house again. The very thought made my blood boil. If I'd been standing in front of it, I could've happily set a match to the place. All the work I'd done to make it the perfect haven from his busy career, and how had it served me? He was out fucking other women.

Nice, Charlie. Real nice.

Inwardly, I seethed, suddenly remembering the little things I'd given in on when we built the place. I'd let *him* make the choices about paint and furniture. The giant leather sofa that I hated in the family room was *his* idea. Sky-fucking-blue paint everywhere in the kitchen, breakfast nook, and sun porch—again him. *"We live on a lake,"* he'd insisted. *"Blue is a lake color."*

I'd wanted a red and yellow kitchen, something French and kitschy, and maybe soft sage green on the bead board walls in the sun porch. But we did it Charlie's way. We *always* did it Charlie's way.

At the time, I was glad to do it because it made him happy and that was all I ever wanted—for Charlie to be happy.

Only the master bedroom was me—soft English chintzes,

painted furniture, and pale green walls—Charlie *gave* me that room to decorate as I pleased because he said it made him feel like he was sneaking into a boudoir whenever he came into it. I bought it, hook, line, and sinker.

Bastard. You still won, even when you made it seem like you were doing me a big favor.

"Mom?" Kevin's foot brushed my leg under the table.

"What?"

"Are you even listening to me?" A frown furrowed his brow.

I nodded. "I was just thinking about what you were saying."

"What was I saying?"

"You think I should sell the house. That it's too big for me to live there alone."

"Yes, but what else did I say?"

"Um…" He had me.

"Meg and I want you to move here." He gave me the little coaxing smile he'd undoubtedly learned at my knee.

"Honey, I don't know—"

"No, listen, okay? It makes perfect sense." Elbows on the table, he leaned in to explain. "You can sell the house and use the money to buy an apartment near us. They're not nearly as expensive as they used to be. Prices have come down in the Bay, too, you know. Then you'll be close to us and to Eddie. Ryan and Renee aren't settled yet and if you're with us, maybe they'll decide to come out here instead of moving back to Michigan. We can be together again."

I could see how badly he wanted me to say *yes*, but it would never work. Maybe I was ready to sell Charlie's dream house on the shore, but I had no desire to move to California.

"Kevin, slow down." Reaching across the table, I covered his hand with mine. "I love you. You and Ryan and Renee are my heart. I miss you every day, but I can't move out to California."

"Mom—"

I stopped him with one raised finger. "This is *your* life. My life's in Michigan. My friends are there. If I moved at all, it'd be to Carrie's old apartment."

I had no idea where that had come from, but it was brilliant. I'd love to live in Carrie's apartment above the boathouse at Dixon's Marina. Then another possibility occurred to me.

"Or maybe I'll move to Chicago, but it's too soon to even think about that."

His chin dropped and I tilted my head to stare into his eyes. Disappointment turned them darker blue. "Can't you at least consider it?"

"I don't need to consider it." I patted his hand. "But I'll be out here so often, you'll be sick to death of me. I've got a new grandson to spoil and I intend to be a world-class spoiler."

The look he gave me told me he didn't intend to give up. "You should check Dad's frequent flyer miles and see if they're transferrable to you. I bet they would be."

"Yeah, I'll check into that." Suddenly a huge yawn consumed me. "I'm tired. Are you ready to go?"

"Yep, I feel like I could sleep for a week." He caught the waiter's eye and air-scribbled, indicating he wanted our check. "Hey, have you seen Will Brody? Liam said he was in Chicago, setting up the summer tour. Glad there's somebody there you kinda know."

"I do see Will now and then. He lives in the same building." No need to expand since I had no idea how Kevin would react to the news that his mother had slept with the man in question. Except for the shiver of sensation the memory inspired, I still hadn't decided how *I* was reacting to it.

At first, my initial response to finding Charlie's secret life was to do the same thing to him—find someone else and fuck his brains out. It was simply about revenge. In that moment of insanity, I believed sleeping with Will would somehow hurt Charlie.

But revenge got lost almost from the second Will's lips touched mine. And now, longing for Will was jumbled in my head with anger at Charlie. The two things had gotten connected in my brain —and in my heart—and I had to disconnect them before Will and I went any further.

If Will and I went any further.

But, at that moment, talking about him with my son wasn't even an option.

I changed the subject. "Tell me about work. How's it going?"

He took the bait, and as we waited for our check, he caught me up on his job and his business travels. I couldn't help chuckling. The kid had no idea how much Eddie was going to change his life.

CHAPTER 14

Exhaustion crept over me as I slid the key card into the mechanism on my hotel room door for the third time. I never could get those damn things to work on the first try. Finally, the light glowed green and I shouldered the door open, dropping my purse, jacket, and suitcase on the small sofa in the sitting area before flopping onto the bed. Blowing my bangs off my forehead with a long exhale, I stared at the ceiling.

I'd forgotten how much work a newborn could be. The cold brewing in Meg when she'd gone into labor had turned into a full-on case of the flu. Chest congestion, fever, coughing, and body aches kept her in bed and miserable while Kevin and I tended to baby Eddie and set up the nursery. The doctor encouraged her to continue breastfeeding and that task took all her energy, so I was teaching Kevin how to change diapers and bathe and dress his new son. In between, we finished the painting and decorating in the baby's room. Despite limited contact with his ill mom, Eddie was a thriving, happy newborn and already cooing and cuddling at only a few days old.

I'd been sleeping on their sofa for several days and longed for a real bed, so when Meg finally started to feel human again, I came back to the hotel for some much-needed solitude. Almost too tired to move, I dragged myself up long enough to yank back the bedspread, drop my clothes on the floor, and fall on to the crisp white sheets. More than anything I wanted about ten hours of uninterrupted sleep. But I'd barely closed my eyes when someone tapped on my door.

What the hell? It's after ten.

All I could think was something had happened to Meg or the baby. But why hadn't Kevin simply called?

Naked, I padded to the sofa and ransacked my suitcase for my short white robe. "Who's there?" I called, pulling it on and tying the belt.

"The big bad wolf," a deep familiar voice answered. "Open up."

Will!

I yanked the door open to find him grinning at me, one elbow resting on the doorjamb, and a duffle in his other hand. Blond hair tousled, five-o'clock stubble on his cheeks, and clothes slightly rumpled, he looked fabulous. Instinct took over and without even thinking, I launched myself at him, throwing my arms around his neck. Dropping the duffle, he enveloped me in a hug as he shoved the door wider and kicked the bag into the room ahead of us. My feet dangled a couple of inches above the carpet when he swung me around, while at the same time, using one foot to slam the door shut.

Like long-lost lovers, we clung to each other before Will's mouth found mine. His tongue probed, and I willingly opened my lips to him. All clear thought vanished. Dear God, I'd forgotten the magic of the man's kisses, the delicious male scent of him. I was a woman possessed, tugging at his jacket, pushing it off his shoulders. He shrugged and it fell to the floor even as I began unbuttoning his shirt.

Releasing me, he yanked it off, heedless of the last couple of buttons popping onto the carpeted floor. I wanted him naked, to feel his big body against mine, so my fingers worked on his belt buckle while he slipped out of his shoes and socks. Cursing my fumbling hands, I tried to unbuckle his pants, but he took over, dropping his pants and knit boxers in one swift movement. His erection jutted out at full attention.

Somehow, everything slowed down. Will's blue eyes darkened in the dim light of the room. Shadows danced from the city lights outside the curtained window. He reached for me, letting one hand slip under the belt of my robe, pulling me closer. Silently, he untied the sash and slid one hand inside, stroking the skin of my waist. Dropping his head, he pushed the robe aside and explored my neck and shoulder with his lips. A shiver of sensation raced through me as I ran my hands over his chest and then around to the muscles of his broad back.

I pressed my lips to his neck, inhaling the warm skin there, teasing with my tongue. Will responded with a growl, letting his own tongue trace a wicked path down to my breast, sucking hard, driving me right to the edge with his tongue circling my nipple.

The robe went the way of his clothes as he suddenly scooped me up and laid me on the bed. "Don't move." The first words he'd spoken since I'd opened the door were soft and husky.

An unnecessary admonition if there ever was one—I had no intention of moving, not when ecstasy was only moments away. My body was on fire, every nerve tingling. I needed him inside me. The zipper of his duffle sounded loud in the dim quiet of my room, and in no time, he was next to me again and his hands cupped my breasts, his blond hair tickling my chin. Thrusting my fingers into his hair, I pressed his head to my flesh, encouraging him to take me into his mouth.

He obliged, sucking and tonguing first one hard nipple and then the other while I squirmed underneath him. Reaching between us, I wrapped my hand around his erection, savoring the silky taut skin. I tugged slightly and opened my thighs, but Will was in charge. He slid down my body, dropping warm lingering kisses over my stomach and lower as I released him.

A moan escaped as he kissed the inside of my thigh, the back of my knee, my ankle, and made his way back up the other leg. Hot, sexy kisses left me breathless, unable to contain the sounds of pleasure. When he moved higher, when he found that special place between my legs, when his tongue stroked there, I bit my lip to keep from crying out. Tension wound tighter in me as Will's fingers gripped my thighs and his lips worked magic. My fingers splayed in his hair. Fire licked at my nerves and my hips rose to meet his hungry mouth. Then everything inside me exploded in a kaleidoscope of sensation. I clutched his shoulders and whimpered.

Before I had a chance to fall back to earth, Will rose over me. Scarcely aware of the faintest sound of foil tearing, I kept my eyes closed until he came into me, hard and hot. When I opened them to his passionate gaze, I clutched.

Oh, God, this man owns me. He owns *me.*

It was my last coherent thought before his lips came down on mine and flames seared through me. His kisses tasted of mint and whiskey and me. The combination intoxicated my senses as I wrapped my arms and legs around him.

His movements were gentle at first, long strokes inside me, pulling away oh-so-slowly while his blue eyes stayed locked on mine. Aware of every inch of his skin, I touched him shamelessly, stroking his back, sliding my heels up over his thighs to his butt, arching into him. I couldn't get close enough even though we were as close as two human beings could be. Heat flared again between my legs, radiating out as he filled me. With a groan, he moved faster and faster still. Sensation washed over me as I clung to him, riding out his climax before mindless ecstasy claimed me again.

Will's naked body shivered now and then—probably more from post-orgasm aftershock than from the cool air—as I lay curled against him, my head resting on his chest. His heart pounded under my cheek. We still hadn't exchanged so much as a hello.

At last, he tipped my chin up to look into my eyes. "Hi, I'm Will. I'm with the hotel." That earned him a smile, so he continued. "I actually only stopped by to see if you needed anything. Extra towels? Another packet of coffee? Perhaps a toothbrush?"

"So you make the rounds with a duffle bag full of condoms each night?" I played along, loving how his blue eyes twinkled in the sparse light from the French doors.

"Well, we here at—" he grabbed the courtesy card off the nightstand and squinted at it, "—um… ah, the Dragonfly, always put our guests' needs first. Our mission is to make sure you're comfortable… and satisfied."

"Mission accomplished." I rose up to press my lips to his.

He kissed me gently. "How's it going, beautiful?" he whispered as I pulled back to gaze into his face.

Beautiful? How easy would it be to fall in love with this guy?

I gave him a grateful smile. "I'm okay. Really tired."

Snuggling back in his arms again, I told him about Meg's illness and how Kevin and I had taken over newborn duty. "She's finally strong enough to be out of bed, so I came back here to try to get some rest." I finished around a giant yawn.

"And I came and disturbed you. Sorry about that."

Tendrils of my hair clung to his stubbled chin, so I smoothed it away. "Honey, you can disturb me like that anytime, but"—another yawn—"I do need some sleep. I don't think I've slept more than about three hours at one time in a week and a half."

"Go to sleep." He stroked down my arm and tugged me closer before tucking the sheet and blanket more snugly around us.

"But… but…" My eyes closed and I struggled to open them again. "I wanted to… to talk."

"We'll talk in the morning." He pressed a kiss on the top of my head "Goodnight, love."

Love…

I was too sleepy to respond.

Morning brought a chill and little fingers of fog through the open balcony door of my hotel room. Will slept soundly. Not even the clanging of the cable cars bothered him. Glancing at the clock on the nightstand, I saw that it was after eight. I hadn't slept in that late since I'd arrived in San Francisco, thanks to little Eddie. Another cable car clattered by, causing Will to roll over, clutch the blanket, and murmur in his sleep. Cautiously, I slipped out of bed and shut the French doors to the balcony, pausing behind the drapes to peer out into the busy street below.

The city was waking up. Business people strode up Powell, a line wound out the door of the coffee shop across the street, and the fog lent weird auras to the streetlights. Naked, I padded across the Oriental rug to the bathroom, waiting to switch on the light until I'd shut the door.

The hotel was old-fashioned and charming—a throwback to the early nineteen hundreds but with twenty-first century amenities such as central heat and air, small sitting areas, king-sized beds, and en suite baths with huge showers. As I washed my face, cleaned my teeth, and ran a brush through my hair, I recalled the last time I'd stayed at this hotel… with Charlie. Will and I had made it our own last night, but still, I wanted to find a place that was *ours*—not some place that might always remind me of *him*.

Slipping back under the covers, I curved my body around

Will's, laying one arm across his hip, and pressing my breasts to his back. He sighed and rolled over, but didn't wake up. His arms slid around me, and he tugged me close with a satisfied moan. I buried my face in his chest hair, letting the warm masculine scent of him fill my nostrils, then ran one finger down his body to his navel.

Is this man my destiny?

He was wonderful, but I didn't know if I was ever going to be open to love again with so much anger inside me. Even lying here in his arms, the rage began to drop a red veil in my mind. I simply had to get past it. Find a way to forgive Charlie, and move on—whether it was with Will or someone else or all alone. This anger would turn me into a bitter old lady, and I didn't want to be that person. I'd come too far in the past few weeks.

But how could I ever let it go?

CHAPTER 15

T he scent of freshly brewed coffee pulled me from sleep and when I opened my eyes, Will stood over me with a cardboard tray from the coffee shop across the street. A waxed paper bag dangled from his other hand, no doubt some delectable treat from the shop's bakery.

"Rise and shine, beautiful. You damn near slept the morning away." He put the tray on the nightstand and sat on the edge of the bed to open the bag and wave it under my nose. "I've got raspberry croissants and hot coffee to get you started. Once you're showered, we'll find brunch somewhere."

"You're one of those chipper pain-in-the-ass guys in the morning, aren't you?" I grumbled, rising up on one elbow to accept a container of coffee and sniff it.

White chocolate mocha!

The man was my hero. I pulled back the tab and took a sip. *Delicious.*

"Hi." I gave him a smile.

Holding the bag out, he leaned in for a kiss. "Hi."

"I'm so glad you're here." I took another sip. "Want to spend the day in bed with me?"

"Sounds perfect, but…" Will's serious expression sent a chill down my spine. "… um…we need to talk."

What on earth did he need to talk to me about? Could he be done with me already? Surely he wouldn't have made a trip halfway across the country to tell me he no longer wanted me. A phone call would've taken care of that. Besides, last night, the passion in his eyes left no doubt about his feelings. No, it was something else, something he was worried about, something he knew I didn't want hear.

Oh shit, he's going to tell me he's serious. He's going to ask me to move in with him.

My heart dropped to my metaphorical socks.

"Will…" I sat up and tucked the sheet around my naked body, trying to think of a way to tell him I wasn't ever going to make another commitment, not after what the last one had gotten me.

Memories had assaulted me most of the time I'd been with Kevin and Meg, watching the tender way my son took care of his wife and new child. Remembering Charlie's caretaking of me when Kevin was born and then again with the twins had brought a sharp stab of pain, even as I rocked baby Eddie.

And it was all a lie.

No. No more marriage for me. I'd been a fool for too many years. All I wanted from now on were easy, fun, no-strings relationships. Marrying so young, I'd missed those. Friends with benefits sounded just about right.

"Wait." Will handed me a croissant on a napkin. "I have something I need to say, so eat and listen, okay?" Perched on the edge of the bed, he was obviously nervous, as he took a long pull of his coffee and shredded, rather than ate, his pastry.

I waited, nibbling on my croissant. Whatever it was, he was having a hard time getting started, and my heart sank even further. It couldn't be good news if he was having such difficulty spitting it out.

"I did something you're not going to like," Will said at last and when he met my gaze, his blue eyes were dark with emotion.

"What?"

"I… I went into your laptop and read Charlie's emails."

"You *what*?" I dropped the pastry next to my coffee on the nightstand. Anger boiled up. "What the hell, Will? When? You had no right to do that. I—"

"Wait." A jerk of his head indicated the laptop open on the table across the room, exactly where I'd left it several days earlier. "I did it just now. I was only going to check the Asian markets, honest. But, there it was, and I've been worrying about why you wanted to bring his laptop along after you told me to throw it out. I know you, Julie. You're going to try to figure out who she is, aren't you?" It all came out in one long breath.

"So what if I—" I bit back the question before I said something I might regret—a rant was imminent. I was so pissed I wanted to smack him.

"Will you just listen before you blow up, please?" Fists clenched, he gazed at me steadily.

Too late!

Through gritted teeth, I agreed with a short nod, but I was seeing red. I couldn't imagine what possible explanation he could have for invading my privacy. Snooping into things that were absolutely none of his business.

"I read them because I could tell you were curious about that woman, and I thought maybe I could figure out her identity. And if I found her and you knew more, you could sorta resolve things in your head." When I didn't respond, he went on. "I thought I could figure out what was going on."

"I fucking *know* what was going on."

"Listen!" Will's voice hardened. "He was cheating on you, that's a fact. But there's more to this than simply Charlie's being unfaithful."

"And how do you know that, *Dr. Phil?*"

He was getting irritated too, but I honestly didn't care. At the moment, I had no more use for Will Brody than I had for Charlie Miles. Was he trying to defend him?

Men suck.

I was done. I tossed the covers off, rose, and stalked around the bed to grab my robe off the floor next to Will's big feet. When I'd tied the belt snug around my middle, he took my arm.

"Come on. Sit and listen. Please." The words were measured and quiet, his expression intent.

Against my better judgment, I agreed and tossed myself down on the loveseat—no way was I going to sit on the bed next to him. I needed space. "Okay, I'm listening."

"First of all, I didn't read *all* the emails, but it was obvious this woman wasn't just his lover, she was his friend. And from what I could tell, they'd been friends for a very long time —years."

"Oh, great. So he was screwing around on me for *years*. There's good news. Thanks for sharing."

"Julie, shut up. I'm trying to tell you—"

"*What?* Don't tell me to shut up. You're the one who's out of line here, not me."

He sat quietly for a few moments and then said, "Please, listen." His calm was more irritating than if he'd fought back.

I was mad—furious, actually—and about six seconds from kicking his ass over the balcony. "Why? What does any of this have to do with *you* anyway?"

With a sigh, he rose and came to kneel next to me. "Julie, you're beautiful and warm and smart and full of life and good-ness. But now there's a dark angry place in you. You have every right. But if you don't deal with it, it's gonna grow into a twisted ugly thing, and eventually it could destroy all the joy in your life."

Damn him.

He was right. He said exactly what I'd been thinking less than twelve hours earlier, but that didn't assuage my anger. This was something *I* had to work out, and Will was getting too close. Charlie's infidelity was something so personal I hadn't even talked to Carrie about it yet.

"This isn't any of your business." I bit my lower lip to keep the tears at bay. Crying was how I'd always handled anger.

Out of the blue, it occurred to me that Charlie had known that and used it to his own advantage too many times in our marriage.

Well, those days are over.

This was a new Julie Miles—no tears. Pissed was pissed and I could rant or scream if I wanted to. Nobody was going to jolly or cajole me out of it, not even a charmer like Will Brody. It didn't matter what he had to say. "You should just stay out of it, Will."

"I can't." He peered down into my face. "I'm not defending him, but maybe you *do* need to find this woman. Learn the whole story. If you don't deal with it and find a way to forgive him and let it go, you'll never be open to loving again. You'll carry that angry baggage around with you for the rest of your life and become one of those bitter old man-hating widows." He made a sour face to demonstrate, but I wasn't amused. "*We* can't go anywhere until you finish all the crap with Charlie."

"*We?*" Okay, so he'd found the one thing to say that stopped me cold. The anger suddenly dissolved into incredulity, and my heart started to pound. I stared into his eyes, dumbfounded.

"Did you think I was kidding when I told you I've wanted you since the first time I met you?" he asked. "Baby, I was a goner from the moment you came down the hall in that stupid hat." He gave me a smile that sent a spasm of sensation through me. "I think I might be falling in love with you, Julie."

"Will… I—"

"Shh." He touched my trembling lips with one finger. "You don't have to say anything right now. As a matter of fact, I don't want you to. I'm not asking you for anything, honest. Right now, I'm asking only one thing of you." He paused, his eyes burning into mine. "If you have to do this search, don't do it alone. Let me help you. Please?"

CHAPTER 16

A small part of me was still reluctant to dig into Charlie's extramarital escapades. But once we got started, it seemed as if I was on a mission—unwilling to stop until I'd found out every available detail about EJT. Will had unpacked his iPad and was researching how to chase someone down using only an email address. We sat across from one another at the small table in the hotel room, both glued to our electronics. I'd calmed down a little in the shower. Although I still resented Will's intrusion, he *was* only trying to help me, and I was clueless about how to find someone on the Internet.

His declaration earlier had set me back on my heels. Confused, flattered, and pissed—all at one time—I was a mass of emotional turmoil. We'd skipped brunch and just nibbled on the croissants while we started our search. I wasn't at all sure whether I really wanted anyone else on this journey or even what I intended to do with whatever we found. So instead of giving into the urge to scream or cry, I worked at remaining detached as I read the emails searching for clues. I pretended they were nothing more than a novel I'd picked up. It was the only way I could cope with the contents.

The notes were intimate, full of sensual innuendo and even outright hardcore, graphic sex. These two people were on fire for each other and that was a fact.

But Will was right; it wasn't just about sex. They seemed to care a lot. The messages weren't only about how much they missed being together and screwing each other's brains out, although there was plenty of that. They were also in-depth descriptions of their everyday lives. Frequently, Charlie talked about me and the kids, but in a loving way, with no indication that he was unhappy with our marriage.

It was kinda weird. In one note, he'd be writing about how much he wanted to be sucking EJT's breasts, then in the next, he'd be telling her about a picnic and bonfire on the beach with the family. Sometimes the tone of the emails sounded as if he were writing to an old friend rather than a lover.

EJT's notes to Charlie were similar—an email full of hunger for him with explicit descriptions of how she wanted to pleasure him was followed by a note detailing a weekend spent camping at Yosemite with some guy named Peter. And I couldn't figure out who the hell Peter was. *Husband? Son? Friend?* Whoever he was, Charlie obviously knew him because he asked about him once or twice with a chatty, *hey, how's Peter doing?*

Intrigued and fascinated in the same manner I'd be mesmerized by some bizarre film noir, I kept reading the emails until I finished them all. Apparently, the two lovers had met a few times a year, but she never came to him. He always went to her, no doubt using the "medical conference" excuse to me. According to their notes, they sometimes talked on the phone, usually when Charlie was headed home late from the hospital, but basically, their relationship appeared to be confined to the few days a year they spent together.

The oddest thing was that they both seemed perfectly fine with the situation the way it was. Oh, there was sincere longing for one another, a lot of *I miss you*, and they both clearly looked forward to their trysts. But never in any email did they mention having a life together—almost as if they had an unspoken agreement *not* to discuss the possibility of leaving their spouses and families to run off and start a new life.

How on earth does that work?

I didn't realize I'd said it aloud until Will looked up from his iPad. "How does what work?"

"None of these emails talk about them leaving their families to be together." I tapped one finger on the edge of the computer. "Don't you think that's weird?"

"I think the whole damn thing is weird." Will nodded and then gave me a hesitant smile. "Hey, can I ask you something?"

I wasn't sure whether I wanted him to, but he was already onboard. I'd granted him admission to this gig, and I believed him when he said he only wanted to help me. I didn't imagine he was taking any kind of sick pleasure in Charlie's fall from grace. I inclined my head slightly.

"Did you ever suspect?"

"No." The word was out of my mouth before I even thought about it. I stretched, arching against the back of the chair and pressing my hands on the surface of the table. Rising slowly, I rolled my shoulders, trying to get the kinks out. "I didn't. Honest. It never occurred to me one time that Charlie would cheat."

Will simply shrugged, turning his eyes back to his iPad.

"What was *that* look for?"

"What look?" He glanced up, all innocence.

"You know exactly what look." I paced the length of the hotel room and then tugged open the French doors to the balcony. It was chilly, but the sun streaming in felt good on my skin. "What are you thinking?"

"Nothing." He avoided my gaze.

"Bullshit." I stomped back to the table, grabbed the iPad, and laid it screen-down on the table. "You're the one who said you wanted to do this with me, so talk to me. You don't believe I never suspected him?"

"No, I believe you." He took a sip from his coffee cup and scowled. It had to be freezing cold.

"Then what?"

"I don't know." He sighed and tossed the cup in the trash. "Maybe this is a mistake. What are we doing, Julie? We could be out exploring the city together right now, having fun. Instead, we're holed up in a hotel room, reading emails between your son-of-a-bitch dead husband and the woman he was screwing. What's the point?"

"Don't call him that, you never even knew him." For the life of me, I couldn't figure out why I was defending Charlie, but my hackles rose anyway.

"Well, what else do you call a man who led a secret life for God knows how many years?" He extended his hand. "Please? Can't you let it go?"

I jerked back, out of his reach. If I allowed him to touch me, I'd lose the fragile hold I had on my self-control and burst into tears. "You're the one who said I need to *deal* with it. That I had to move on. Have you changed your mind?"

"Yes, I don't want to do this. It's a mistake. It's too much. Just let it go."

I didn't want him to feel sorry for me or try to talk me out of finding out who this woman was. I was convinced that if I could see her, maybe I'd understand what had driven my husband from my arms into hers. "I can't. You don't get it, do you?"

"No, I'm sorry, I don't," he confessed, folding his hands on the table. "Frankly, I think the good doctor was an asshole of the first order. He had a charmed life with the most beautiful, wonderful woman in the world, and yet, that wasn't enough for him. What kind of an egotistical dick cheats on someone like *you*?"

His words warmed my heart in spite of the anger I'd been nursing the entire afternoon. His expression said it all. He really cared. He wasn't being charming or trying to flatter me. The part of me that was so drawn to him wanted to agree that Charlie Miles was a big jerk, a stranger I'd never truly known. It would've been wonderful to drop this search and maybe go walk around Union Square or take a cable car to the Embarcadero. But the other part of me, the wounded wife, wasn't going to rest until she knew the truth.

I had to find out who this woman was and what her hold had been.

"But he wasn't an 'egotistical dick', Will. The Charlie I was married to wouldn't have *looked* at another woman." Tears stung my eyes and I blinked them back, determined not to give into another storm of crying.

"Then who's *this* guy?" A nod gestured to the laptop on the table before us.

"I don't know." I caught my lower lip between my teeth to keep it from trembling and regained control. "I don't know. Maybe if I find *her*, I'll figure out why—why he—"

"Christ!" He stood and stalked to the open doors, gazing out at the busy street below, then spun around. "He was a narcissistic jerk, Julie. That's *why.* What happens when you find this woman? You gonna bitch slap her or something? Then it can be all *her* fault, and you can love Charlie again? Put him back up on the pedestal?"

His remark hit so close to home, I reeled. "What an awful thing to say."

"Sorry." Will was immediately contrite, coming over to pull me into his arms. "I'm sorry, Jules." One hand smoothed up and down my spine as the other cupped the back of my head. He pressed his lips to my forehead. "I'm trying here. I want to understand."

"It's not about putting Charlie on a pedestal." I leaned back in his arms, my palms against his chest. "It's about the last thirty-two years of my life. I–I can't bear it if those years meant nothing. If that's true, who am I? Don't you… don't you see?" The words caught in my throat as my gaze captured his.

With a groan he leaned down and his lips found mine. After a sweet slow kiss, he lifted his head. "I hate that bastard. If I could beat the shit out of him right now, I would."

He released me, reached for the iPad, pressed the Home button, and held it up. "Her name is Emily Tucker. Her family owns Tuckaway Winery."

Emily Tucker? Unbelievable!

Blood pounded in my ears as I shook my head, trying to clear it enough to comprehend what he'd said. I felt behind me for a chair and dropped into it, feeling sick to my stomach. Charlie had loved that winery. Raved about it all the time. Special ordered their wine because it wasn't available in Michigan. God, how many times had we toasted anniversaries and birthdays with Tuckaway Petit Syrah? A bottle of their Riesling was always chilled in our wine cooler. It had been our summer go-to wine after a long hot day on the beach.

Suddenly I felt light-headed as I remembered all the times Charlie and I had taken that particular wine to bed with us, sharing a glass as we snuggled together after sex. I put my head down between my legs, taking deep breathes to keep from losing the croissants and coffee.

How could he? How could he pour *her* wine for me, toast me, lick it out of my navel, and be diddling the winemaker?

"Hey?" Will's hand was warm on my shoulder. "You okay?"

I raised my head to meet his concerned gaze, and nodded, giving him a grim smile. One more deep breath and I turned to the laptop, typed "Tuckaway Winery" in the search box, and found the website. Now I was even more determined to see her.

I was disappointed to see there were no pictures of Emily Tucker, only photos of the vineyard and winery. Googling her name didn't bring any photos I thought could be Charlie's little paramour either. What I found were a bunch more shots of the winery, bottles of wine, and folks picnicking in the Sierra foothills at Tuckaway. The faces in the pictures were too tiny to see much, just happy, laughing people enjoying a day of wine tasting. Charlie wasn't in any of them. Frustrated, I tapped one nail on the table, trying to come up with a better way to search for her.

His face unreadable, Will sat opposite me before hopping out of his chair and pushing the lid down on the computer and shutting the iPad. "Come on, get dressed." He took my hand and pulled me out of the chair. "Let's go find some real food. We need to get out of here."

I was dying of curiosity and could've spent the rest of the afternoon and evening scouring the Internet, something I wasn't about to admit to Will. The confession would've only incited another *Dr. Phil* moment, so I went along.

CHAPTER 17

I slipped my sunglasses on against the glare as we drove Will's rental car east into the foothills the next morning. He'd balked strenuously about driving up to Angel's Camp, but I was adamant. He could come with me or not, but being so close, no way did I intend to miss an opportunity to at least try to get a look at Emily Tucker.

Tuckaway Winery was beautiful and aptly named, set among the foothills and surrounded by vineyards. I could see why Charlie had loved it. It was his kind of place, simple, elegant—a beautiful, cedar structure that oozed money and taste. After we parked, Will turned to me, leaning one arm on the steering wheel. "Are you sure you want to do this?"

Without a word, I bolted from the car and stalked to the open door of the winery, wishing alternately that the tramp would be there so I could ream her out, and that we wouldn't be able to find her so I'd never have to face this other woman in my husband's life.

The building was old and immaculately restored with a high ceiling and huge beams. A fire crackled in the big stone fireplace, while an older woman and a young, very attractive brunette poured tastings for a few people lined up at the bar.

Hesitating in the doorway, I sensed Will behind me. One hand on my shoulder, he guided me into the winery, and I leaned into his touch as we approached the tasting bar. The brunette set two glasses in front of us along with a wine list.

"Welcome to Tuckaway. Are you tasting with us today?" she chirped.

When I didn't respond, Will nodded and picked up the sheet. "Yes, please."

"Where would you like to start?"

"What do you recommend?"

"Depends on what you like." She brushed her long hair back from her face and leaned in to display her sizeable rack to the guy *I'd* come in the door with.

Very professional, you bimbo.

Was *this* the woman? Had to be, the way she immediately started coming on to Will. She'd seemed kind of young at first, but up close, lines around her eyes told me she was north of thirty-five. Besides, didn't most men go for younger chicks when they strayed? I glowered her, trying to picture her with Charlie, before saying with a snarky undertone, "Give me some Riesling. My *husband* used to love your Riesling." My voice came out too loud, echoing in the cavernous room.

Will nudged me with his elbow.

I shot him a frown. "What?" I asked, again too loudly, but I didn't care that I might be embarrassing him. He had to have figured out this was Emily Tucker. Hell, any idiot could see she'd be the type to screw someone else's husband.

"Let's start with the drier sauvignon blanc first," he suggested, giving me wide eyes, apparently trying to send some kind of signal I wasn't particularly interested in receiving.

By that time, a couple of the people who were down the bar

stared at me openly. I turned my back on them and pretended to study the wine list. "I want the Riesling, dammit."

"Jules, chill." Dull color rose from his collar and he took a sip of wine, clearly unhappy with my attitude.

"Here's the Riesling." The girl poured some into the glass in front of me. "We can start wherever you like."

"How gracious of you." I slugged the wine down and put my glass back on the counter none too gently.

"Would you like to try our Vignoles?" The brunette eyed me with caution.

"Why not?" I eyed her right back, determined to make her as uncomfortable as possible.

"Thanks, Emily. See you in a month." One of the other couples called out as they headed for the door.

Swinging around, I gaped as I realized I'd picked the wrong woman as the conniving harlot who'd had an affair with my husband. My jaw snapped shut as Emily Tucker approached, a pleasant smile on her lined face.

"Hello. How are we doing today?"

This was Charlie's lover? This round, plain woman who appeared as though she could be someone's grandmother. When I glanced up at Will, he gave me a raised brow before settling a supportive hand on the small of my back. Shocked speechless, I couldn't begin to muster the scorching words I'd practiced in my head in the car. I simply stared at her.

The woman wasn't what I'd expected. My imagination had run riot since I'd discovered Charlie had been unfaithful, picturing a curvy brunette, a tall sexy redhead, or a tiny bosomy blonde. They'd all been young and dumb, and in my mind, I'd cut them down with one contemptuous glance. But *this* woman? What was the attraction? I couldn't imagine them having a cup of coffee together, let alone fucking each other senseless. No way was she even close to the type of woman Charlie had typically found attractive.

Or… or maybe she was, and *I* was the one who wasn't a good match.

But we were a great match for over thirty years. Weren't we?

My mind whirled with images of my handsome husband and Emily Tucker, but I simply couldn't make them fit. Finally, I cleared my throat. "Are you Emily Tucker?"

"Yes, I am."

"Do you know who I am?" My throat tightened again, making my voice gravelly.

"Yes, I do." With a quick gesture, she and the brunette switched places, and she reached under the bar and poured white wine into our glasses from a chilled bottle. "This is our Vignoles. The grapes are from our vineyard in the central valley. It's crisp and light. Think grilled salmon on the patio on a summer evening—maybe a salad and some sourdough bread." Her rote speech came out way too fast.

I found my voice, although it sounded strangled. "Really? *That's* what you have to say to me?"

After gazing at me for a long moment, she came around the end of the bar. "Why don't we talk outside on the deck? The view's wonderful and it's warm today."

I saw she was wearing worn leather sandals with her gypsy skirt—she had the smallest feet I'd ever seen. I followed her out the side door while Will hung back at the bar. I scowled at him over my shoulder and gave him a head jerk and a glare, but he stood still and simply sipped his wine.

Now *he leaves me alone. Bastard.*

"Have a seat." The woman moved with surprising grace, her skirt flowing around her trim ankles as she pulled chairs out at one of the tables and extended a hand in invitation.

I sat across from her, unable to stop staring at her short,

severely styled gray hair and dated wire-rimmed glasses. I'd prepared a venomous attack in the event I got to speak to Charlie's lover, but the words had vanished. The whole scenario was so surreal I couldn't think of a single intelligent thing to say.

"Doc talked about you often and showed me pictures. I knew who you were as soon as you walked in." Emily folded her arms and rested them on the table. "How did you find me?"

Frowning, I leaned back in my chair, powerless to take in the absurdity of the situation.

I'm sitting here with my dead husband's mistress, and she's an old lady.

"Charlie's email." My words were clipped as I began to come back to myself.

"Ah." Her dangling silver earrings tinkled when she nodded her head.

"What the hell did he see in *you*?" The words were out before I could stop them. I was so puzzled by her, by the thought of my Charlie with her, I couldn't have kept from saying them if I'd tried.

She blinked and sat back, running a trembling hand through her hair. The air was crisp in spite of the sun and goose bumps chased up her arm. "I…um…"

Her discomfort sent a twinge of guilt through me. That was below the belt, but it had just slipped out. Besides, look what she'd done to me.

"How dare you?" I leaned toward the table and smacked my palm on the stone surface. "How dare you have an affair with *my* husband?"

"Believe me, I didn't plan it."

"No one ever does, do they?" My voice was icy. "Oh, I know. It just happened? You met and you couldn't resist?"

"Something like that." She rubbed her hands up and down her biceps, the gesture belying her calm tone. "We met at a wine tasting in the city. I was pouring at Emilio's and he came in with a group of other doctors for dinner. We started talking and—"

"Look, I don't need the gory details, okay?" My mind simply couldn't comprehend the fact that she was speaking about *my* husband.

She stopped talking, apparently waiting for me to say something.

The only thing that came to mind was, "How long?"

"Almost sixteen years."

"Why?" I croaked, inwardly cursing my awkwardness. She was so calm, and I felt like a dumb kid in the principal's office.

"I was a widow with a small boy, trying to keep a family business together. I wasn't interested in a relationship, but when I met Doc, we… we just clicked."

My heart began to pound and my palms were sweaty on the arms of the chair. I curled my hands into fists, trying to understand what she was saying. I wanted to scream at her.

He was married! To me*!*

Instead *I* sat waiting this time. I needed to understand.

"For Doc, I think it was that, with me, he didn't have to be… um… perfect."

The words shook me to my core. "*What?*"

"In Michigan, life was a fairy tale. Beautiful wife, accomplished children, lovely home, incredibly responsible job, and a whole community of people who believed he was invincible. It was sometimes overwhelming… being Superman." She shrugged. "Here with me, he was just Doc. He didn't have to be wise or clever or responsible for anything at all. It was wrong and imperfect, but he needed a little imperfection in his life."

Heat began to rise in my cheeks.

Is this woman kidding?

"*That's* your story? Seriously? Life with me was too *perfect,* so he had to start fucking you? Unfreakin' believable." I snorted.

"That's pretty clever. Do you suppose he used that same line with all the others?" I threw my hands up in disgust and started to push up out of the chair. I'd heard enough.

"He wasn't a serial cheater, Julie. There were no others."

"Oh? Would you like to bet your winery on that?"

"In a heartbeat." Her expression remained composed as she gazed at me. "He adored you and he cared for me. He needed you, but he also needed me."

I sat back in the chair, watching her face, the loving light that shone in her eyes as she talked about *my* husband. Her teeth worried her lower lip—it was obvious she was fighting tears. With a shaky breath, she rose, hands clenched at her sides.

"Forgive him, okay? He and I had nothing to do with *your* marriage. I took nothing from you. He worshipped you. I was… an… oasis. Nothing more." She swallowed hard. "If I'd pressed him to make a choice, he wouldn't even have had to think about it. I didn't because I was nuts about him. And I was selfish and willing to take any time I could have with him."

"You're wrong. You took everything from me!" I cried. "You took my life. Everything I believed was true for thirty-two years is gone now, can't you see that? I thought we had the perfect marriage, but—"

"I'm sorry you see it that way, but that's the rub, isn't it? Nothing's ever perfect. You don't have to forgive me, but you need to forgive Charlie and move on. He'd want you to be happy, Julie. It's over. Let it go." She left then, simply walked away.

I sat in the warm afternoon sun for a while, trying to process what had just happened. My husband's mistress asked me to forgive him for cheating—with her. That took class. Maybe I wasn't the only one who'd lost someone dear when Charlie died, and Emily had never even had the chance to say goodbye.

What an inane path my mind was taking. Why was *I* feeling sorry for *her*? My emotions were in such a turmoil, I had no idea anymore what I was feeling. I came to the winery loaded for bear, ready to knock this cheating little bitch into the next county. But I hadn't been prepared for this dignified woman.

When I walked back into the winery, Will was waiting, and Emily was once again behind the tasting bar. As I passed, she inclined her head ever so slightly. I nodded in return and walked right past Will and out the door. But I saw her blinking back tears as she served her customers, and my heart ached a little.

CHAPTER 18

E mily's mournful face haunted me as we headed back to the city.

A fiery sunset painted the sky ahead gorgeous shades of red, pink, and orange as Will and I drove west out of the foothills. The day had worn me out, and I rode silently, watching the trees and rocks go by. My head lolled back against the leather seat as I struggled to keep my eyes open. With a jerk, I snapped to attention.

"We're about two hours from the city," Will said. "Why don't you go ahead and shut your eyes for a while? Get some rest."

"I don't want to sleep," I replied in tone sharper than I intended.

"Well then, just recline your seat a bit and get comfortable."

As he patted my knee, I could see that he was approaching me very cautiously. I hadn't told him anything about my encounter with Emily at Tuckaway, and he hadn't asked.

I took his advice, pulled the lever, and let the seat back. I hadn't been this emotionally drained since the days after Charlie's funeral. The scene at Tuckaway replayed as an endless loop in my head, always coming back to her face, lip quivering, eyes filled with unshed tears.

Why the hell am I feeling sorry for her?

She'd tried to steal my husband. She'd cheated with him for years. She was a whore, a self-centered bitch who had no respect for marriage vows. A home wrecker—

A home wrecker?

The words echoed in my brain. My conscience nudged me.

Whose home did she wreck? And she's no whore, you saw that immediately.

I had to admit that Emily Tucker didn't seem like the kind of woman who'd go after another woman's husband. Any more than Charlie Miles had seemed like a man who'd be unfaithful. If anything, meeting Emily had confused me even more.

Goddamn you, Charlie. You couldn't even screw around like a normal guy. So typical. You had to do it elegant and with someone I might've liked if things were different. You bastard… .

Releasing a frustrated breath, I yanked the seat lever and sat up straight again, focusing on the scenery around us.

"You okay over there?" Will took his eyes off the road long enough to give me a wary smile.

Poor guy. He'd borne the brunt of my wrath since I'd discovered Charlie's secret, and he only wanted to help me deal with it. Wrinkling my nose, I returned the smile. "I've been a bitch to you lately. You're a nice guy, you don't deserve that. I'm sorry."

"What's the old line? Love means never having to say you're sorry?" He offered the infamous words from *Love Story* with a goofy grin.

Laughter bubbled up inside me, and I didn't try to stop it. Catching his eye, I snickered, then let go.

Will cracked up too, chuckling as he drove.

Pretty soon, my sides ached and tears rolled down my face. I had no idea why I was laughing so hysterically, it wasn't even that funny. I gulped in deep breathes trying to control it and before I knew it, the laughter turned to sobs. Suddenly I was weeping uncontrollably.

Will scanned the highway up ahead for someplace to pull over as I lost it in the seat beside him. He took the next exit and careened into a spot in the far corner of a McDonald's parking lot.

As soon as he stopped the car, I jumped out. I didn't get any farther than the front of the car before I doubled over. My heart hurt so bad I was certain it was literally breaking. Finally, I pulled up to a standing position and hiccupping back more tears, rubbed my wet cheeks with my palms.

He leaned against the front fender, gazing at me, his hands fisted at his sides, his expression unreadable.

I took a deep shaky breath. "Sorry." Accepting the napkin he handed me, I blotted my eyes and face.

"No need to apologize." He gave my shoulder an awkward pat, clearly unsure of what I wanted him to do. That uncertainty lasted all of half a second as I launched myself at him and his arms enfolded me.

"Thank you, Will." I twined my arms around his neck.

"For what?" He tugged me close, wrapping his arms around me in the chill of the northern California dusk.

"For… being here. For always being a friend when I need one."

"A *friend*?"

"You know what I mean." Heat suffused my cheeks as I ducked my head.

"Yeah, I guess I do." With the slightest hesitation, he pressed a soft kiss to my lips. When he lifted his head, something almost like sadness showed in his expression. He hurt for me. He really was the kindest man I'd ever known.

I pulled back to rest my head on his shoulder, and we stood

together in the headlights before I drew away to peer into his face. "I need to go home."

"Okay, we're on our way." One last squeeze and he released me. "It'll be a couple of hours before we're back at the hotel." He cocked his head toward the restaurant. "Do you want some food before we hit the road?"

"No, I mean *home*. I need to go back to Willow Bay."

I had to talk to Carrie. If anyone could make sense of the mess I'd discovered, it was my dear friend. The need for her was so urgent, I booked an early morning flight on my phone as he drove us back into San Francisco.

Will was unusually quiet on the ride home, and although we shared the big bed at the Dragonfly, we didn't make love. I left him at the hotel for a couple of hours so I could run by the kids' place for one last snuggle with little Eddie. When I got back, he was sound asleep. In the morning, his manner was casual and friendly—almost, but not quite, distant. There wasn't much time to talk since we both had to be at SFO early, and this new cooler Will only added more confusion to the morass of emotions already swirling in my head. But I pinned on a smile as we drove to the airport and chatted pointlessly about the traffic and fog.

There was no passionate farewell as there had been when I'd left for San Francisco and that puzzled me, too. He was headed to the International terminal to catch a flight for Europe, and still hadn't said a word about what might happen in the future. He didn't even mention calling me while he was away checking out venues for Liam. When he dropped me at the Departures door, we stood on the sidewalk by my roll-on bag, silence yawning between us.

"Um, thanks, Will, for everything." I toyed with the handle of my purse and stared at the travelers scurrying by us.

"Travel safe, Jules." His voice was rough. "I hope you find what you're looking for in Willow Bay."

I couldn't leave it there. I had to say more, even though he was parked in a loading zone and the airport police would be along soon to shoo him on his way. "I'll be back in Chicago in a few days, maybe a week."

"I'm not sure when I'll be back."

"Will…"

When his eyes met mine, his discomfort was obvious. "We both have a lot of thinking to do. I'll see ya, Jules." With that he drew me into a quick hug and left. I had no idea when I'd see him again.

Bewildered and heart-sore, I boarded my flight, determined not to worry about Will Brody. First things first. I had to work my way through Charlie's deception and betrayal before I could even begin to consider anyone else.

The plane circled wide over the lake before making an easy landing on the runway at Cherry Capital. Fidgeting in my seat, I reached in my pocket for my cell phone right as the flight attendant gave the all-clear to turn them on. I wanted off that plane and into the safe haven of Carrie's friendship.

"Jules!" Carrie's voice carried over the heads of the few travelers in front of me. I walked on tiptoe, anxious to catch a glimpse of her, and in only a few seconds, there she was, waving and smiling. Tears choked in my throat as I slowed down and swallowed hard, determined not to start blubbering all over her immediately.

"Hey." I released the handle of my carryon to pull her into a big hug. "God almighty, I've missed you!"

"I've missed you too." Carrie returned the embrace with fervor. "I can't believe you didn't give me any warning, you big dope." She continued as we separated and headed for baggage claim. "How many bags do you have?"

"This is it." I gazed at my old friend, who looked fantastic in snug jeans, a plum-colored turtleneck, and a leather jacket.

"But… where's all your stuff?"

"In Chicago. I only laid over there. I'm actually coming from San Francisco. Will dropped me at SFO this morning."

"Will?" Carrie eyed me quizzically, then grinned when I nodded. "I think we're going to need chocolate and alcohol for this. Car's in the garage. Come on." With a little head jerk, she led the way, not saying any more until we'd stowed my bag in the back of her SUV and were both belted in and on the road.

"Can I stay with you?" I knew the question would surprise her since I hadn't had a chance to tell her anything at all since Eddie's birth except to phone that I was on my way.

"Absolutely," she replied without a moment's hesitation. "That's probably better. Liam's been stripping wallpaper in your bedroom, getting ready for the painter. He's over there right now, vacuuming and trying to get things cleared away enough for you to settle in, but you staying with us is a much better idea. The painters can get started right away."

Laying my head back against the headrest, I closed my eyes.

"Hey, we're here." Carrie's soft voice pulled me out of the stupor I'd fallen into as we drove from the airport to George Street.

Liam appeared on the big wraparound porch, looking tall and handsome in plaid flannel and denim. I didn't even let my eyes go next door to my house… *Charlie's* house. At the moment, I couldn't bear the sight of it.

"Hey, Granny, congratulations. You look like a million bucks." Liam greeted me with a hug and took my carryon, hauling it easily into the house as he followed us in.

I knew without glancing behind me that they were exchanging one of those married-people looks that said more than words, because he headed upstairs to the guest room with my suitcase while Carrie took my coat.

The scent of coffee filled the air, and when we got to the kitchen, two mugs, cream, sugar and a bottle of Jameson sat on the counter. A fire crackled on the hearth of the two-way fireplace and a new chintz overstuffed sofa crouched in front of the flames, looking cozy and inviting.

With a grin, I held my arms out as if to embrace the whole room. "You made your keeping room." I toured quickly through the kitchen, past the tall stools at the breakfast bar and then around the sofa. Carrie had created a charming scene, with a couple of small side tables, an armchair, soft lighting, and Liam's collection of antique toy tractors on the mantle. "I love it. It's perfect."

"It came out nice, although Evelyn's grousing because I turned the breakfast nook into a sitting area and now we eat at the bar." Carrie poured coffee into the mugs. "Every time she comes to clean, she just shakes her head and mutters under her breath." She held the bottle of Jameson over a mug, a question in her eyes.

Just then, Liam sauntered in, hands in his pockets. "Aha, you found my treat. Pour some in for her, honey. The sun's over the yardarm somewhere."

My heart swelled and my eyes stung. Could there be two dearer friends in the whole world? "You guys are the best," I managed, swallowing hard to keep the tears at bay.

By God, I'm not going to weep through the telling of this. Only the facts and without histrionics.

Frankly, I was bored with my own tears at that point. I'd cried so much over Charlie Miles, I was sick to death of my own pathetic affect.

Liam fetched a can of whipped cream from the fridge and topped our coffees off before giving me a wink. "I'll leave you two to your catching up."

"No, wait, please." Suddenly I wanted a man's perspective… well, the perspective of man who wasn't in love with me. "Stay. You may as well hear this firsthand."

"You sure?"

"Absolutely."

With a quirked brow at Carrie, who shrugged and nodded, he poured another coffee, doctored it up and settled on the sofa with one arm around his wife. I curled up in the armchair next to them, warming my hands with the mug.

"Where's Izzy?" I realized I hadn't seen hide nor hair of their four-year-old adopted daughter. Usually Isabella was bouncing around my knees, lisping and giggling.

"She's down at Noah and Margie's for an overnight." Liam sipped his drink. "I dropped her off after Carrie headed to the airport. Thought maybe you and Carrie might want some time alone."

"This guy's a gem, Caro. Hang on to him."

"Do you see anything to indicate that I'm *not* hanging on?" Carrie gave me a smile as she leaned her dark head against Liam's shoulder.

"Not really." I tasted the whipped cream with the tip of my tongue. The scent of coffee and good Irish whiskey filled my nostrils. For the first time in longer than I could remember, I relaxed, letting the warmth from the fireplace seep into my tired body.

"How's it feel to be a grandma?" Carrie snuggled closer to Liam. "Are you freaked or delighted?"

"Or both?" Liam added. "We saw the pictures on Kevin's Facebook page—damn good-looking kid, Julie."

"Being a grandma rocks. He's a sweetie." I sipped my coffee, letting the whiskey give me the courage to share my story. "I–I need to talk."

"Julie, what is it?" Carrie reached out a hand to me. "What's going on?"

Taking a deep breath, I dove in, telling them the whole story from the moment I discovered the emails between Charlie and Emily to the encounter with her at Tuckaway. I left out the intimate parts between Will and me—those were still too new to share. I wasn't about to say anything in front of Liam about going across the hall in my rage over Charlie's infidelity and practically attacking his best friend. He'd never get it and would probably worry about Will getting hurt. No, that was for later, when Carrie and I were alone.

They sat silently as I spoke, shock and concern evident on both their faces. Finally, when I stopped to take a breath, Carrie rose from the sofa to kneel on the soft rug in front of me.

"Oh, Jules, I'm so sorry," she said, cupping my face with one hand. "What an awful discovery." Sympathy tears shimmered in her eyes. Pure Carrie Reilly—aching for me as I knew I'd be aching for her if our roles were reversed.

I nearly lost it at her touch, but I bit the inside of my lip and set my jaw, firm in my resolve not to cry. I wanted to talk, to get some input from a more objective source than Will, to try to make sense of the bizarre twist my life had taken. I put my hand over hers and linked our fingers as I gazed into her face.

"Well… so what do you think?"

CHAPTER 19

"*Sixteen* years?" Liam repeated for the third time.

"Yup."

We were on our second cup of Irish coffee, and I lapped at the froth floating in my mug, feeling rather proud that I'd managed to contain my tears. Fact was the urge to cry simply dissolved as I hashed out the story with Carrie and Liam. It was almost as if I was talking about a stranger rather than my husband of over thirty years. Yes, I was still hurting, but I was gaining perspective.

"God, I couldn't be more shocked if you'd told me *Liam* was having an affair." Carrie had settled back on the sofa. "This feels completely out of character for the Charlie Miles I knew."

"Something was obviously missing—something he needed that I couldn't provide."

"Don't!" Carrie said sharply. "Don't take this out on yourself, Julianne Miles. This was all about *Charlie*. He was weak. You were a brilliant wife. You made him the perfect home."

"Apparently, *that* was the problem. Life was *too* perfect." I couldn't help the snort of laughter at the ridiculousness of those words. "I made him feel like he had to be perfect, and he couldn't handle it."

"That's the dumbest thing I've ever heard." Carrie swatted the idea away with the back of her hand. "Too perfect? For God's sake, honestly—"

"Hang on a minute, honey," Liam interrupted with one hand on Carrie's thigh.

"You better *not* be thinking about defending him, Liam Michael Reilly!" Carrie swung around to glare at her husband. "What he did was unspeakable!"

"Chill, babe. You're right. That's not where I'm headed." Liam gave me a long look. "Jules, Charlie led a charmed life— dynamic, successful career, gorgeous wife, beautiful, smart kids, great friends—and he always had to live up to the image he created. I know how it feels to try to be something you're not."

"Are you seriously going to try to compare *your* playboy life before me with Charlie's screwing around on his wife?" Carrie's eyes were huge and her voice squeaked. "Did *you* know already? Did he confess this to you on the golf course or during one of those 'boys' nights' on your boat?"

He tossed her a quick scowl. "Of course not. I'm as shocked as you are."

I considered jumping in to head off a marital spat, but I was curious as to where he was going. I'd asked him to stay, believing I wanted an objective man's viewpoint. Liam and Charlie had become good friends in the last few years. Perhaps the Maestro had insight.

I gave Carrie a head shake. "Go on, Liam."

She threw herself back against the sofa cushions with a frustrated little sound, crossing her arms over her chest and tapping her toe. My dear friend was clearly in full-on outrage, undoubtedly furious with Charlie because he'd hurt me. But Charlie was dead. She had nowhere to put the anger, so she turned it on Liam.

I could identify. It's difficult to be pissed at a dead man. I was still hurt beyond words, but talking it out had lessened my anger considerably.

"What I'm trying to say," Liam continued, "is that it's hard to be someone you're not, even if you're in the midst of a life you're proud of and enjoy. It's not easy to become a celebrity in the world of classical music, and I loved the whole image of being a famous conductor. Hell, I *still* love it. But the persona *I'd* allowed to be created around me? Not the real me. The harder I tried to live the way I thought I should, the worse I felt." He paused and glanced at Carrie out of the corner of his eye.

She sat in stony silence, obviously not prepared to give him one moment of quarter. All I could think was that he'd better get to his point fast or he'd be sleeping over at Noah and Margie's with his daughter tonight.

"Charlie wasn't—what was the word that woman used?" Liam raised his hands, palms up. "Superman? But that's how all of us saw him and it's how he saw himself. We depended on him to be a super hero. He thought he was."

"But *he* created that." Carrie turned her whole body on the sofa to face him. "*He* did that. We didn't ask him to be Superman. Julie never wanted him to be *perfect*. She loved him just the way he was."

"Perfect," I whispered.

"What?" She swung around to me. "What did you say?"

"Caro, I see it. I hate it, but I kinda see what Liam's saying." I stared at him. "I fell in love with this guy who worked so hard to be everything to everybody. Because he seemed so perfect, I worked hard, too, being exactly what I knew would make him happy and proud. I never once asked myself, *What do I want?* Always, always the question in my mind was, *What does Charlie want?*"

"So he repays your devotion by finding another woman and

screwing her brains out for sixteen years?" Carrie's voice rose another octave. "How in God's name are you making *that* work?"

"Do you know that I used to get up really early and do my face and hair and then go back to bed and wait for him to wake up?" My mind was reeling and I knew I wasn't making sense, but I had to process all of this mess, so I went on relentlessly. "He was a morning man, and I didn't want him to have sex with someone who wasn't... perfect. *Both* Charlie and I worked so hard to create and maintain that fairy tale life. No fucking reality.

"Charlie never once had to *ask* for so much as a coffee refill, I was always right there, anticipating his every need. I got up with him each morning to brew coffee exactly the way he liked it and make breakfast, always elegant in my designer jogging suit or a silk nightie and robe. My hair was done, my makeup flawless." I bounded out of the armchair, moving restlessly around the room. "Shit, Charlie never even felt razor stubble on my legs—I kept myself smooth and gorgeous, right down to the French bikini wax *he* adored, but *I* hated." I grimaced. "Sorry, Liam—that's probably TMI."

"No problem." His teeth gleamed in the lamplight.

"I didn't do the Paris and New York shows, which could've put my career into orbit, because it might've interfered with *his* life. And I loved going out on gigs—it was the only time I got to think about just me. But I never pursued anything more than the catalog stuff. Instead I stayed right here, being... I don't know... June goddamn Cleaver. Charlie built the perfect house for his perfect wife and kids and installed us there, while he went off to his perfect job of saving people's lives. And he got to be the hero of the world."

"Dammit, Jules, if you say *perfect* one more time, I swear I'm gonna smack you!" Carrie pressed her stomach against the back of the sofa, having turned and risen to her knees to follow me as I paced.

"But that's it, don't you see?"

"No, I don't see anything except you trying to take responsibility for Charlie's awful behavior."

"Liam, *you* see, don't you?" Beseeching, I turned to him.

"Honey, I think what she's trying to say is Charlie created such a fantasy that he couldn't live up to it after a while, and yet, he couldn't destroy Julie and the kids by *not* being that guy." Liam put one hand on the small of Carrie's back as he explained. "The other woman was a place to decompress. A poor choice, obviously."

"Why are you two making excuses for him?" Carrie slammed her palm on the sofa and expelled a frustrated breath. "What he did was *wrong*! He cheated. He took something he'd promised only to you and gave it to another woman."

The irony of the situation struck me, and I couldn't help grinning at her. I'd come all the way to Willow Bay so my best friend could talk me through *my* anger and pain, yet sweet, tenderhearted Carrie was the one who was furious and unforgiving. *I* was the one trying to be understanding of what Charlie had done.

"But, it didn't affect my life one bit, Caro." Even as I said it, I realized the truth of it. "He was still a wonderful husband, and he loved me."

"He *did* love you," Liam said. "He was crazy about you. You could see it every time he looked at you. More than once, he told me how lucky he was to have you."

"Thanks for that, pal." I walked around to perch on the coffee table in front of Carrie as she sat back down. "Realizing that I couldn't be everything he needed hurts beyond words. But I bought into the *Leave It to Beaver* scenario, too. I never stopped to ask if our life was what he really wanted. Hell, I never stopped to wonder if it was what *I* really wanted. We started it and it took off—a fantasy marriage that ate him alive."

"So, that's it?" She sank back, glaring first at me and then at

Liam. "We chalk this all up to poor old Charlie having too much *perfection* in his life and let it go?"

"No." I knit my fingers together in my lap, struggling to find the words I wanted. "I have a lot of thinking to do. Why didn't he feel he could come to *me* when he got overwhelmed? I've got to try to figure out what I might have done differently, so I don't make the same mistake again. If I ever have another opportunity—"

"I hate that bastard," Carrie burst out. "You're beautiful and wonderful and good, and he made you doubt yourself. I *hate* him for that. Why didn't he delete all the damned emails?"

"I imagine because he didn't expect to die so suddenly," I replied with a little shrug. "Part of the Superman complex. Charlie was gonna live forever, "It's done now, Caro. But you know one thing that Emily said really stuck with me."

"What was that?" Liam had embraced Carrie again, stroking her arm, soothing her anger. It was working. She'd settled back against him, curled up next to him like a kitten.

"She said, 'I took nothing from you.' At first, I was floored and furious. I couldn't believe she said that. But you know what? She was right. I had everything—my marriage, my kids, my beautiful home, and Charlie's devotion."

"But, he wasn't—"

"No." I raised one hand to stop Carrie's denial. "Don't you get it? As far as *I* ever knew he was completely devoted. She *didn't* take anything from me at the time."

"What about now? What about all the memories she's tainted?"

"I was the one who went looking for her. As far as she was concerned, it was done." I shook my head with a small smile. "Those memories are *mine*, Caro, not hers. She can't ruin something she was never a part of. Don't you see? If I let over thirty years of wonderful be destroyed by this news, then that's a choice

I make. And why would I do that to myself? That would just be stupid."

"And that makes it all okay? You decide to let this go and Charlie's still the big hero?"

"No." Wrapping my arms around myself, I scooted closer to the fire. "No, Charlie's still a cheating son of a bitch. But he's dead. I can wallow and spend the rest of my life hating him. Or I can square my shoulders and get on with my life. This time I get to choose."

An unfamiliar, but suddenly empowering sense of self-assurance surged through me as I stared into the flames.

"*I* get to choose."

CHAPTER 20

I opened the gate and stood staring at the big beautiful house that Charlie Miles built. The clapboards were damp from the frost melting off the roof in the morning sun. The yard was covered in a thin layer of late winter snow. A piece of screen that had pulled loose from the enclosed back porch flapped in the breeze.

Charlie and I had talked about needing to fix that tear when we'd been at Mackinac Island over a year ago. It had been on his *honey-do* list, along with repairing the broken drawer handle in the powder room, redoing the master bedroom closet, and replacing the drain cover in the basement laundry room. None of it ever got done.

Stomping snow off my fur-lined boots as I entered the porch, I saw that someone—probably Carrie—had removed the cushions from the wicker furniture and rolled up the woven rugs. Charlie and I had spent many a summer night on this porch, snuggling on the settee, sipping wine, and listening to the sound of the waves on the shore far below.

Nostalgia welled up in me, but to my surprise, not melancholy. Instead I smiled at a vivid memory from years ago. Our eight-year-old twins, their faces grubby, careening into the screened porch with a jar full of lightning bugs one dusky July evening. Charlie had helped them punch holes in the jar lid with an ice pick, so the bugs' lighted tails could be a lantern for a while. He'd always had time for the children, ready to wipe snotty noses, help build a soapbox derby car, explain a tricky math problem, or cuddle away a nightmare. He'd been a stellar dad. No one could deny it.

When I shouldered open the back door to the house—it always stuck in the winter—the scent of fresh paint smacked me. I gasped. Apparently, Liam had kept the painters busy in the kitchen as well as in the master bedroom because Charlie's lake-blue kitchen was now soft pale yellow. The old dark oak cabinets gleamed white in the morning sun, freshly painted and bearing new pewter hardware. It was gorgeous. Carrie's handiwork, I was sure. As I removed my down jacket, I smiled at how well my dear friend knew me.

The yellow walls continued into the breakfast nook where they'd painted the plantation shutters white as well. The round oak pedestal table had been replaced with a glass and bronze pub-style set, and the built-in corner cupboard also bore a new coat of white paint. With a bright red-and-yellow rug on the hardwood floor and cheery red and yellow flowered cushions on the tall chairs, the entire effect was cozy, French, and totally me.

I wandered slowly through the rest of the downstairs, trailing my fingers over the leather sofa, opening the blinds, straightening a crooked lampshade. Someone had cleaned recently—every surface was dust-free. Each room held memories of Charlie. His office off the family room where I could visualize him sitting at his massive mahogany desk, writing articles for some medical journal. The sofa where he'd spent rowdy Sunday afternoons with Kevin and Ryan watching football, basketball, baseball—whatever sport was in season. The dining room where we'd served so many holiday meals together, toasting friends and family and stuffing ourselves silly.

Upstairs, I followed my nose to the master bedroom, which reeked of the primer the painters had applied the day before. The room was in complete disarray. Furniture was shoved into the middle of the room and covered with a giant drop-cloth, the bed was taken apart, and the mattress and box springs were nowhere to be seen. The wallpaper had been stripped and stuffed into trash bags that were neatly lined up in the hallway, and when I peered into the guest room across the hall I found the contents of my closet.

Charlie's belongings had disappeared. Nothing of his remained except for a few of his favorite t-shirts and sweatshirts that Carrie had folded into a box and labeled it for Kevin, Ryan, and Renee. I reached for the faded *MSU Dad* hoodie that was on top, hugging it to my body, and holding it up to my face to inhale the scent of my husband that still lingered in the fabric. Shivering in the cool air in the house, I slipped into it, enjoying the feel of the soft cotton, the sleeves that fell past my fingertips, and the way it seemed to embrace me.

Gingerly, I stepped over three gallons of paint, bending down to see what colors Carrie had chosen. Soft taupe with a lighter cream for the trim. *Nice.* The windows were bare, blinds and curtains removed for the painters. Far below, I saw the lake, grey and restless in the early March breeze. Morning sun glistened off the whitecaps as they rushed onto the beach.

Perched on the wide windowsill, I leaned back against the frame to gaze out at the world that had been my whole life for so many years. We'd had a good life together, Charlie and I. Raising our family in this beautiful place was exactly what I would choose again given the opportunity. Would I make any changes if the Universe gave me a do-over? Certainly.

I'd be more assertive and less accepting—ask for what *I*

wanted now and then, rather than always deferring to Charlie's desires. I'd take the Paris gig and put off the babies for a couple of years. I'd bag some of the hospital social stuff—the cocktail parties, the fundraisers—stop worrying about being the perfect hostess and spend more weekends on the beach with my kids.

I'd make my husband talk to me, tell me what was in his mind and heart instead of simply expecting him to always be there, ready to take on whatever life presented next. Maybe I couldn't have prevented him from straying. I'd never know for sure. But perhaps he would've been less inclined if we'd all—including Charlie himself—expected less super hero and more just plain Charlie.

And yes, I'd choose Charlie Miles again, in spite of what I'd learned recently. The pain of discovering his affair had subsided to a dull ache that I knew one day would probably fade into a distant sad memory. Until then, I needed to concentrate on my life in the here and now—where *I* was going, what *I* wanted to do. I straightened to standing, stretching with a big exhale before removing the hoodie and placing it back in the box for the kids.

It was time to let this old house go, pass it on to a new family who'd make their own wonderful memories here. The thought of putting it up for sale didn't even make me particularly sad. I only hoped it would sell quickly. For the rest of spring, I'd stay in Chicago, continue with the therapist, and keep working at La Belle Femme. There was the fashion show to put on, and Sarah had talked about expanding the shop into the empty storefront next door. I'd already started decorating the new space in my head.

When summer arrived, I'd talk to Noah about renting Carrie's old apartment above the boathouse—the place Will stayed when he was in Willow Bay. Maybe we could share it. The anticipation that surged up inside me that thought, waned immediately. Will was well across the Atlantic by now in some exotic city. Was he thinking about me? Wondering if I was okay?

Maybe.

Maybe not.

Something had changed. In no time at all, he'd taken hold of my heart, and then backed away with alarming speed. I had no idea what had cooled his ardor. Maybe it finally hit him that I was a *grandmother*. Perhaps he simply decided he wasn't up for the drama of a menopausal woman with so much emotional baggage. I'd scared the poor guy off, and that realization left a lump in my throat. It wasn't anything I could fix right now though, and I had one more important stop to make before I headed back to Chicago.

~

I steered Liam's little Mercedes roadster through the rows of headstones, driving slowly along the narrow road. Carrie had objected when I asked to borrow a car, saying that I wasn't emotionally ready to handle a trip to the cemetery.

Liam stepped up, tossing me the keys to his car before I could even open my mouth to argue with her. "Go on, Jules. We'll be here when you get back." He'd given me that million-dollar smile as he put an arm around Carrie, whose dark eyes were so full of worry.

I kissed his cheek, then hers, and headed out.

Charlie's grave sat on a hill near the back of the cemetery in front of a line of pine trees. I'd picked the spot myself, knowing it didn't matter where I put the shell that was my husband, but also oddly convinced he'd enjoy the view overlooking the town and the bay. Parking by the side of the road, I wrapped up in the knitted scarf Carrie had shoved at me as I left, and then I pulled on my gloves. The sun was still high in the sky, and rivulets of water from the melting snow ran down the road by the grass.

The black granite headstone gleamed, drawing me as surely as if Charlie himself had been lounging there, crooking his finger at me. I imagined him as I ambled past the other graves, picturing that leonine mane of grey hair, that cocky tilt to his chin as he gestured, *Come here, babe.*

The Christmas greens were gone, cleared away by the grounds crew so the grave looked stark.

I should've brought some flowers.

I dismissed the twinge of guilt. This wasn't *that* kind of visit. Kneeling down by the marker, I brushed some stray pine needles away from the base. Engraved letters stood out above the dates in the black stone and I traced them with one gloved finger.

Dr. Charles Edward Miles
Beloved Husband, Father, Son

"You son of a bitch," I said, sounding almost conversational. "What the hell, Charlie?"

I plopped down on the concrete in front of his grave, heedless of the damp seeping into my jeans. Legs folded meditation style, I crossed my arms under my breasts and waited for the tears, the words of recrimination I'd planned to say, the anger I'd expected to dump here. But none of that happened. For a moment, my mind was an utter blank, then what came out of my mouth shocked me right down to my socks.

"Remember the day we made love in the lake? You told me that stupid story about the plaque on the lighthouse that had the pairs of initials on it? You said the initials were carved there by men who'd managed to get and keep a hard-on in the icy waters of Lake Michigan? Oh and use it as well?" I grinned at the memory, stroking the headstone as if it were alive and able to respond to me. "We swam all the way out to the second sandbar. I laughed so hard I almost choked when you dropped your swim-suit and put my hand down there to prove to me you could do it.

"Then you gave me that look"—I closed my eyes, picturing his face, those sultry eyes that burned with desire every time he gazed at me—"and my bikini bottoms practically fell off, I was so hungry for you. And we did it. Do you remember? Do you remember how glorious that was? How free we felt? Making love in the lake in the middle of the afternoon when the kids were at school and the beach was empty."

Opening my eyes, I stared up at the wispy clouds floating across the clear blue sky before speaking again with a chuckle. "You laughed your butt off when I wanted to go up and add our initials to the plaque. I was so disappointed to find out you'd made up the story, so you took your Dremel tool and carved our initials in the big rock at the bottom of our beach steps. *A new tradition*, you said. And it made me feel better. We never did find the swimsuit. Remember? You had to go all the way back up to the house and get me a different one. God, I damn near turned into a frozen prune waiting on you." My heart sped up at the memory of that happy day—just one of thousands I'd spent with this man.

"I should hate you, Charlie. For just a little while, I *did* hate you." Lacing my fingers together I leaned my elbows on my knees and rested my chin on my hands. "I could've lived the rest of my life without knowing you'd fucked around and been perfectly happy with my naïve memories. I even invented a story like the ones you were so good at creating. I figured maybe you *wanted* me to find those emails so I'd stop putting you a pedestal and find love again. Move on with my life." I snorted a laugh, shaking my hair back off my face.

"Well, I'm fairly confident it was nothing more than you being so cocksure about your own immortality that you didn't believe you needed to delete them. I'm sure you never imagined

I'd discover your secret life or that you'd die before you could erase any traces of it."

Anyone who drove past me in the cemetery probably thought I was tragic figure, sitting there on the damp concrete, talking to a headstone. But I didn't care. The catharsis was too sweet.

"And if you think I'll ever apologize to you because you didn't find everything you needed with *me*, you're crazy. I owe you *nothing*. I gave you the best life I knew how to give. Tough shit for you if it wasn't enough." I rose, brushing the back of my jeans with both hands before laying my palms on the top of the stone.

"But I forgive you, Charlie. I can't be bitter and sore for the rest of my life, so I forgive you. There's still an evil part of me that no longer wishes you'll rest in peace. Frankly, I'm kinda hoping you're squirming up there in the hereafter, wracked with guilt and feeling pretty goddamned awful. Not forever, mind you, but for a little while—just until *I* get up there and can smack you senseless."

I patted the polished surface of the marker. "So long, Charlie."

CHAPTER 21

Standing among the boxes and crates in my living room, I once again thanked the heavens for Carrie's unnatural proclivity for organization. She'd come into the house armed with packing supplies, stickers, tags, and a clipboard. In less than three days, I was damn near ready to go. Most of my clothes and shoes were either packed to go to Noah's or already at the charity store in town. I'd even shipped a bunch of stuff to La Belle Femme, including a couple of small tables for decorating, a whole box of costume jewelry, and two boxes of scarves and pashminas.

How in the hell did I acquire all this stuff?

Dumb question. Charlie Miles had shopped with passion and panache. He was the shopaholic in our house and loved to pick out everything from dishes, to candles, to my clothes. He'd always had in his head exactly how he wanted me to look and could go into a boutique or department store and dress me from head to toe. The hell of it was he was invariably right. I looked like a million bucks at every fundraiser, cocktail party, and event we attended. I glanced down at my grimy sweatshirt and yoga pants with a rueful smile.

"I can just hear you now, Charlie," I whispered as I taped the last box of knick-knacks and wrote *Charity* across the top in bold black letters. "If you saw me like this, my hair in a ponytail, covered in dust, you'd be appalled and swoop right in and carry me to the shower. Then you'd find something slinky and sexy for me to wear and we'd head to town for dinner. The whole time you'd be scolding me, telling me I should've hired someone to do all this."

But I was glad I'd decided to dig in and do the work myself—it gave me a real sense of accomplishment and independence. I wandered among the boxes and furniture, amazed at how much I was letting go of—how little I was taking with me. I'd already signed a contract with the realtor, and the house was going on the market next week. The tag sale would be in mid-April, and Noah and Margie had enthusiastically agreed to rent Carrie's old place above the boathouse to me on a six-month lease starting in June. If I hadn't figured out what I wanted by Christmas, I'd sign another lease and keep trying.

The new pub table was going with me, along with the wicker from the screened porch, furniture for a guest room, and about a third of my dishes and kitchen supplies. Otherwise, I was going shopping, a thought that filled me with delight. *My own furniture!* I anticipated scouring magazines and shops to find exactly the right pieces.

"Julie, what about the attic?" Carrie's voice wafted down the stairs.

Shit! I'd forgotten about the attic. I charged up, taking the stairs two at a time and met her in the hall outside my bedroom. Entrance to the attic was through the walk-in closet. Together, we scanned the detritus of thirty years, all carefully arranged throughout the huge space above the garage, thanks to the ever-vigilant Dr. Miles, who'd shared Carrie's organizational skills. Dusty boxes were labeled according to which child's mementos were inside, furniture from past years occupied one corner, and

Charlie's and my childhood stuff was boxed and neatly labeled in another.

I will not be overwhelmed. I will not be overwhelmed.

I repeated the mantra I'd been saying to myself since we'd started this project. Then I made an executive decision, something I'd become quite brilliant at in the last few days. "Boxes go to storage until the kids can come and sort through them. Everything else, we'll put in the sale."

"Even the antiques?" Carrie quirked one dark brow. "Your mother-in-law's antiques?"

"Aw, damn. No, wait." I chewed my lower lip for a second. *Damn.* Charlie's mom and sisters set a huge store by the family antiques. They'd been the topic of more than one heated discussion between Charlie and his overbearing twin sisters. I knew my kids would never be interested in the hulking pieces. "Okay, I'll call the wicked sisters and tell them to come and get whatever they want. No doubt they will. Jane's been resentful about that damn grandfather clock since Gerta gave it to Charlie twenty years ago. Not a single holiday passes that she doesn't mention it in a snarky tone." I snorted a laugh. "That's actually why he put it up here and covered it with a dust sheet, so he wouldn't have to hear about it every time she came over. It didn't stop her, by the way."

"I wondered why it disappeared from the dining room." Carrie's eyes twinkled as she scribbled on the clipboard. "Okay, antiques to wicked sisters, boxes to storage, everything else to the tag sale."

She put an arm around me when we turned to go back downstairs. "I'm so proud of you. A few months ago, you never could've done this. But here you are, kickin' ass and being deliciously ruthless."

"Yeah, well…" I gave her sidelong glance. "Surprising how easy it is now. It's only stuff and most of it, not even *my* stuff."

"Can I say something?" Carrie turned to me at the bottom of the stairs, hugging the clipboard to her chest. She had that sheepish yet sly smile that always preceded her dabbling into areas of my life I hadn't opened up to her—yet.

"You can say anything at all, you know that. Absolutely *anything*." I suspected she was about to bring up Will Brody, and her next words confirmed my suspicions.

"I don't know what's gone on with you and Will, but—" Brow furrowing, she hesitated. "He's a great guy and I think he's—well, I think he might be falling in love with you."

"That's what he said." Our eyes met as we plopped down on the steps for what was destined to be a very personal conversation.

"God, are you kidding? He said that?" Carrie's face was wreathed in smiles. "Seriously?"

"Right before–before we went up to the winery." My face heated.

God, how juvenile—this is my dearest friend. We can talk about anything.

Carrie clearly didn't miss the blush on my cheeks because she gazed at me affectionately. "Have you been doing the nasty with our Will?"

I couldn't resist chuckling. After all the times I'd wheedled and cajoled intimate details from her when she and Liam first got back together, I figured I owed her a little dish. "Yep."

"When?"

"The night I found out about Charlie," I admitted with a grim smile. "And again when he came to San Francisco."

"Are you shitting me? And you never said a word? I'm seriously pissed." Her grin belied her words. "So tell me everything!"

"I'm not proud of this, Caro. I went down to his apartment in a red rage. My only thought when I knocked on his door was *fuck you, Charlie, I'll show you screwing around.* It wasn't my finest moment…" My voice dwindled off as I remembered grabbing Will's shirt and kissing him senseless and how the heat exploded between us almost as soon as my lips touched his.

"I hear a *but* coming. I certainly hope you're about to tell me the whole thing turned into *his* finest moment."

I sighed, resting my elbow on my knee with my chin in my hand. "I'd never had sex with anyone but Charlie—and he—he made me, you know… feel great. But, I kinda—kinda—" I grasped for the right words. "—always held back a little. Do you know what I mean?"

"I'm not sure. I think so." Her teeth worried her lower lip. "The couple of times I tried it before Liam and I got back together weren't all that great. But Liam? He turns me inside out." She blushed herself and gave a little shrug. "He makes me completely mindless."

"Mindless," I repeated. "Yes. Yes, that's it. That's what happened with Will. Once he started touching me, I was a goner. In less than two minutes, I'd totally forgotten my mission. All I wanted was Will, and it had nothing whatsoever to do with Charlie. I was right there and dear merciful God, it was *amazing*."

"Well, that's good, isn't it?"

"I don't know. Life's been so screwed-up, and my anger at Charlie is all mixed up with—with whatever it is I feel for Will. I've got to sort it out, Caro, and I don't have that first clue how to begin." Staring down at my stocking feet, I wriggled my toes. The mere thought of sex with Will brought heat and damp between my legs, something that had never happened with my husband. Oh, we'd gotten to the heat and damp, but it took some effort on his part. I could barely fathom how simply picturing Will's surfer boy good looks accomplished the same effect.

It wasn't just sex though. Will's kindness, his sense of humor, his intelligence, and patience—they all made him damn near irresistible. I hadn't stopped thinking about him since the day I visited Charlie's grave. But I had no idea whether he was even interested anymore. It certainly hadn't seemed like it when we'd parted two weeks ago at the airport. "I'm not sure he still feels that way."

"Why?"

"He was, I don't know, different, when we went our separate ways." I shrugged. "Friendly and kind as always, but a little distant."

"Are you in love with him?"

"I don't know. What kind of judge am I? I've only ever loved one man in my whole life." I folded my arms under my breasts, shivering in the chill air in the house. "Besides, I'm too old for this starry-eyed, ain't-love-grand crap."

"Bullshit!" Carrie's eyes flashed with indignation. "You're never too old to be starry-eyed, and Will's certainly worthy of a few stars." She gave me a frown. "And just for the record, love *is* grand."

"You should know." I nudged her with shoulder.

"You bet your scrawny ass, my friend. You know, I think you're handling all this stuff really well." Carrie rose and, offering me a hand, she pulled me up from the stair. "So relax and let the relationship with Will work itself out. If it's meant to be, it'll work. Don't overthink it."

"His very words."

CHAPTER 22

"Well, we're getting closer. We may actually pull this thing off." Sarah's eyes shone as she waved me over to the computer in the back room of La Belle Femme and pointed to the spreadsheet she had open on the screen. "We've already sold eighty percent of the tickets to the fashion show, which covers all the expenses of putting it on, plus enough extra to stay afloat here another three months. That's assuming our jackass of a landlord doesn't raise the rent and the utilities stay in their current neighborhood."

"I'm so glad!" Actually, I was beyond glad, I was overjoyed. In the two months I'd been back in Chicago, we'd put all our energy into planning and promoting the fashion show, which was going to be at the end of May at the Stamford, an elegant old hotel on Michigan Avenue. The hotel had contributed the venue, while dozens of Carrie's and my friends had donated designer clothing from their own closets.

Our twist was that everything we used in the show would go up for auction that night. It was an opportunity for all those society folks to exchange designer labels without actually having to go down to a resale shop. In moments of utter immodesty, I thought it was a brilliant idea and apparently I wasn't the only one. Between ticket sales and the auction items, chances were good we'd rake in enough money to keep the shop running for a very long time.

Naomi and Carl Fox, the owners of the modeling agency I'd been signed with since the age of sixteen, pitched in with enthusiasm when I told them about the project. They jumped on board with a caterer, carpenters to build our catwalk in the banquet room, an auctioneer, marketing ideas, a band, and best of all, models.

My compatriots, models of all sizes, from petite to plus-sized, were ready to take a walk down the runway to support battered women in the Chicago area. I was so proud of them, mostly because I knew a few of those women had suffered some of the same kinds of abuse. Our cause was close to their hearts, so they were giving it their all, creating a very professional-looking show.

"This couldn't have happened without you, Julie." Sarah tossed me a smile before she went back to the computer. "You've been such a blessing here, I don't know how we're going to manage when you go back to Michigan."

"I love helping out. It's been good for me—keeps my mind busy, and I'm having the time of my life putting this show together."

My words were true. The show was the only thing keeping me from dialing Will daily and begging him to get his butt back to the Windy City. I hadn't heard a word from him. I'd considered texting him, but I couldn't do it. Considering how we'd parted in San Francisco, I'd feel like a fool, but I did put his name on the guest list for the fundraiser. Last I'd heard from Carrie, he'd been in Budapest, inspecting venues and meeting with artistic directors and publicity people, getting Liam's tour together.

I wanted to talk to him, see each other face-to-face. The chemistry that suddenly felt off since our trip to Tuckaway was still in full force though, because I was longing for him. That part of me that wanted to charge ahead to see what was possible between us grew more insistent each day. Several times, I'd written him long emails, pouring my heart out, telling him that I still believed in happily-ever-after, in spite of everything. Charlie's betrayal hadn't crushed my spirit or my desire for love. I wanted to try again—with him. Then I'd reread them and hit Delete, feeling like a silly teenager with a crush on the high school football star. Was it too soon to love again? If he still wanted me, would my sore heart allow me to love Will freely? I had no idea. All I knew for sure was that I missed him like crazy.

I sorted through another garment bag of donated designer clothes from yet another of Carrie's society friends. Donations were coming in faster than we could unpack them after she'd put the word out about our show. I'd managed to pull at least one outfit, sometimes several, from every person's collection. I wanted to have fifty great looks for the show. But the bag I was into now took my breath away.

"Sarah!" I exclaimed, holding up a shimmering pink silk chemise gown covered in glass beads. "This is a vintage Lanvin! Look at that intricate beadwork."

"Is that a real flapper dress? Is it valuable, do you think?" Sarah had confessed she knew nothing at all about fashion, but she clearly recognized the dollar signs in a vintage couture gown.

"I imagine it's *very* valuable. We can check online." I was busy taking cleaner's plastic off another dress. *Another vintage gown.* "This one's a Worth, bias-cut." I held up the cream silk crepe evening gown. "Looks like it might be from the thirties. Oh, Lord. Is this seriously a Fortuny jacket?"

"Huh?" Sarah came over to examine the articles as I laid them out on the table. "A who? What?"

"Mariano Fortuny. He was a Spanish designer in the twen-ties." I ran a hand lovingly over the material of the jacket. "He did a lot of experimenting with dye and block prints on fabric. Just look at these colors."

"How do you know all this stuff?" Sarah lifted the jacket and slipped her arms into the sleeves. "You said you never went to college."

"I didn't." Turning her around to face the mirror behind us, I fussed with the jacket, arranging the mandarin collar, pulling her red hair out of the back to let it lay over the grass-green printed fabric. "I've always been fascinated by fashion, so almost everything I read is about fashion—history, biographies of designers, magazines. There." I gave her shoulder a little pat. "That looks fabulous on you, Sarah. You should keep it."

"It *is* gorgeous." She shifted in front of the mirror, trying to get a peek of the draped back. "But if it's valuable and could bring in some cash, we need to include it in the auction."

"There must be at least ten items in this bag." I pulled other articles of clothing out of the big zippered canvas bag. "These vintage clothes shouldn't be on hangers, not even padded hangers. They should be stored flat in special boxes and wrapped in acid-free tissue."

"Who donated this?" Sarah lifted the bag to search for a tag, but found nothing to indicate who'd brought it in.

I scanned the list of names of contributors. Not a clue as to who'd left the large canvas garment bag. It wasn't on the list. "Maybe Holly knows who brought it in. I'll go ask her."

Carefully setting a plastic-wrapped fur on the table, I noticed that it bore an Evans label—one of the premier furriers in Chicago in the 1930s. It looked like black mink. *Wow!* Wandering out to the retail area of the shop to find Holly, I ransacked my memory for what I'd read about Evans furs.

Just as I got to the counter, the front door opened and a male form stood silhouetted in the opening.

"Hello." I backed up. "Can I help you?"

"I don't know. Can you?" He ambled out of the sunlight and I recognized him.

It was Jeannie's husband, Brian. He'd come in once before, crying and trying to find her. Sarah had sent him away with a threat to call the police if he ever showed up again. Her mantra, *don't ever tell them about this shelter*, sometimes fell on deaf ears, particularly if the woman was young and terrified—like Jeannie. They wanted so much to believe their abusers could change. Jeannie had come and gone twice in the short time I'd been working here. We hadn't seen her in several weeks.

I heard a sharp intake of breath as Holly appeared from behind a clothing rack at the back of the store, her eyes huge and her chest heaving.

Stay calm. Stay calm. I repeated the words in my head before I said to her, "Holly, hon, why don't you go start working on those boxes in the back?"

She remained frozen, obviously too terrified to even take a step, so I gave the man my best charming hostess smile.

"What can I do for you, Brian?"

"I'm here for Jeannie." His response was clipped and loud, echoing off the high ceilings. "I know you took her in again. Where is she?" His black hair fell into his eyes as he marched the rest of the way into the store. He wasn't crying now. Dressed in khakis, a blue button-down shirt, rep tie, and a navy sport coat, he could've been any businessman walking down Michigan Avenue, except that his blue eyes were icy, glittering with rage.

I sidled toward the cash register and the alarm button below it, all the while trying to make eye contact with Holly—a futile effort. She was so frightened she stood stock-still with tears coursing down her cheeks. Sliding my hand across the counter, only inches away from the button, I tried to engage the guy in conversation.

"Why do you think Jeannie's here?"

"Now, where else would she be?" Brian's tone was almost conversational, but he eyed me warily. "She came back to her mother's last week, and called me. I took her back home where she belongs. Everything was going so well, but then she disappeared again."

"We haven't seen her in several weeks." I maintained my smile and the eye contact, in spite of the fact that I was sick with fright. Sarah had taught me to look these bastards straight in the eye and never show any fear. No matter how innocuous they seemed, they weren't harmless. They were dangerous.

"You haven't?"

"No, I'm sorry, I haven't." I raised my voice slightly, hoping Sarah was listening from the back and calling the cops.

"You know what? I think you're lying." The charming smile remained as in one swift move, he came at me, grabbing my hand, practically yanking me over the counter. "Don't even think about setting off that alarm. We're aren't finished talking yet."

My astonishment must have been written all over my face because the jerk smirked before releasing my wrist. "Oh, yes, I know all about the alarm button." He sighed and shook his head, giving me a pitying look. "Why do you women always make me resort to this?" Almost nonchalantly, he pulled the biggest damn gun I'd ever seen from of his jacket pocket.

Please, please be calling the cops, Sarah.

Holly's sharp intake of breath echoed in the high-ceilinged shop. I gazed straight into her face, trying to give her some reassurance we'd be fine. Sarah had to be dialing 911 right now.

"Now, tell you what. Jeannie told me about all the phones you keep at hand, so I'm going to need you"—he pointed the gun at Holly—"to collect them up and put them here on the counter. We may be sitting here all day and I'd hate to be interrupted. I can wait forever. She's bound to show up at some point."

Holly bolted to attention when she saw the gun, hurrying

around the shop, picking up the five phones we kept tucked around the store for emergencies such as this one. When she dropped the phones in a row on the counter, I scanned them.

Oh shit. There are six.

That meant that the phone from the back room had gotten left out in the retail area *again*—something Sarah continually scolded us about.

My heart sank. She wasn't calling 911 unless she'd discovered my cell phone on the table where I'd been working, because she'd told me only that morning that hers had gotten dropped in a sink full of water and was no longer functional. We'd even discussed what kind of new phone she should get. I let her play around with mine, which was why it was on the table instead of in my pocket.

"Is this all of them?" Brian waved his gun over the phones.

Nodding, I put an arm around Holly's pudgy shoulders as she sank against me. "We don't know where Jeannie is." I was proud that I kept my voice from quavering. "Honestly."

"Honestly?" He gazed around the shop before backing through the racks to the dressing cubicles and sweeping aside the curtains. His calm demeanor was more terrifying than if he'd been knocking over plants or sweeping the jewelry display off the antique table next to the counter. "What would *you* know about honesty?"

What kind of a sicko remains so composed while holding a gun on two innocent women?

"Brian…" I began, while sending Sarah mental pictures of the cell phone on the table next to the vintage clothes.

"Where is she?" he demanded swinging around to point the gun directly at me.

"She's not here, dickhead." Sarah pulled open the louvered doors that separated the storeroom from the shop, and breathing fire, strode toward the man. "Get your fuckin' ass out of my shop."

"No, I don't think so." The guy turned his attention from me to Sarah, who marched boldly up to him. "Are you really *this* stupid, lady? I'm not falling for that tough chick act again."

Sarah rose on her toes and got right in his face. "I mean it. Get out. Now."

I breathed a small sigh of relief to see the outline of my phone in the back pocket of her slim-fitting jeans. The police *had* to be on their way. But the sigh turned to a scream when the man shifted the gun in his hand and struck Sarah in the head with the butt of it. She folded onto the floor with a thump.

"Sarah!" I cried, trying to shake Holly's death grip from my arm.

"Don't. Don't you fuckin' move." The cruel expression in Brian's eyes sent a chill down my spine as I realized he was losing his cool. This guy wasn't going to be reasoned with or talked down.

I backed up as he headed into the rear of the shop, feeling rage emanating from him when he brushed past me. As he ransacked the place, knocking over boxes and tables in his fury, I made an executive decision.

Sarah was out cold but still breathing. She was okay for now. I knew we had to move immediately. Grabbing Holly's hand, I started for the door, shooting an arrow of prayer heavenward.

Please, please, Charlie, a little help here, okay? If you're still with me, help…

I shoved Holly ahead of me and just as we rounded the end of the counter, I heard a familiar voice say, "Julie? What the hell's going on?"

CHAPTER 23

Will stood in the open door of the shop, looking to my terrified mind exactly like a knight in shining armor.

Will! Thank God!

Charlie, you did it.

The insanity of that thought flitted through my mind even as I grabbed Will's bicep and held on for dear life. How and why he ended up here didn't matter a damn. He was here, and at that moment, I was overjoyed to see him.

"Jules? Are you okay?" His eyes narrowed as he surveyed the scene before him and repeated, "What's going on?"

"There's a crazy guy in the back," I whispered, releasing my grip on his arm. "The husband of one of our girls. He hit Sarah." I pushed Holly past him and out the door. "Go, Holly, now! Meet the police down by Michigan Ave. If you don't see them, run into one of the buildings and get some help. Go!" I turned her in the direction of the street corner and gave her a shove as Will headed into the shop.

"Stay here." He stopped by the counter, head cocked to the side listening to the banging and crashing coming from the back room.

"Will, he's got a—"I came up behind him and peered over the counter to see Sarah moaning on the floor. Her head was bleeding where Brian had struck her. "Oh dear God, Sarah." Scurrying to the other end of the counter, I grabbed a scarf off the display.

Will was hot on my heels.

We knelt on either side of her and he felt for broken bones as I dabbed the wound at her hairline with the scarf.

"Sarah?" Will patted her cheek. "Sarah, talk to us."

"Where is that asshole?" Sarah mumbled, clearly struggling to open her eyes.

Quiet suddenly reigned in the back room, and when I looked up, Brian stood in the doorway, his gun trained on Will.

"Well, this is cozy." Brian sounded calm but the gun wavered slightly in his trembling hand.

"Hey, man." Will rose, his hands out at his sides, palms up. "What are you doing?"

"Trying to find my wife. I know she's here." His eyes shifted nervously from Will to me and back to Will before finally focusing on me. "Give me the key."

"What's your name?" Will edged toward the counter, and I was certain he was trying to draw Brian's attention away from us.

"Why does that matter?" Brian waved the gun in our direction. "Which one of you bitches has the key to the gate?" He referred to the courtyard gate behind the shop. It led to the actual shelter and was kept locked at all times. Apparently, Jeannie had told her husband more about the operation here than we ever imagined. So much for never sharing any information with your abuser.

Damn her.

"His name is Brian Jenner." I stood up and parked myself between the gun and Sarah, who had risen to one elbow and then dropped back down again with a moan. "He thinks his wife is here, but I told him we hadn't seen her."

Still no sirens. Where in the hell were the police?

"Look, Brian." Will leaned one hip against the big glass display case, his elbow resting on the counter near the cash register. I had to give him credit—he appeared way more relaxed than he possibly could've felt. "You don't want to do this. Put the gun down and let's talk."

"I don't want to talk to you, asshole." Brian's face reddened as he dismissed Will with a wave before stepping closer to me. "I want *you* to give me the key."

My heart jumped to my throat as I moved back, almost tripping over Sarah, who was still prone on the floor. "I don't have it. I'm only an employee."

"Liar."

Will eyed the gun and I could tell he was calculating his next move.

I tossed him a panicked glance, begging him wordlessly not to do something stupid. Surely the police would be here any second. We just needed to keep this guy talking. "I'm not lying."

"She doesn't have it." Sarah's voice rose from the floor behind me, and when I looked down, she was sitting up, one hand pressing the scarf to her head. "Only the director has a key."

"Let's go find the director then." Brian grabbed my arm, pulling it up behind me as he spun me around and shoved the gun in my ribs. "Come on. You can help me convince him to open up."

"No!" Will leapt forward with a roar, shouldering Brian away from me while at the same time pushing me toward the counter. I stumbled and caught myself on the edge of the cash register just as the gun went off with a loud pop.

"Goddammit!" Wrestling like a pissed-off bear, Brian took Will down with him as he crashed onto his butt. The gun flew across the room, landing just a few feet from the open door.

The two men scuffled on the floor in the narrow space behind the counter. One of them was bleeding, but I couldn't tell which of them it was. However, Brian was definitely gaining the upper hand as he curled his fingers in Will's blood-soaked shirtfront and punched him in the jaw. Will's head bounced against the wall and he tried to return the blow, but missed, grazing his fist along Brian's shoulder. As I watched in horror, Brian pulled his hand back to strike again.

Oh Jesus, it's Will who's bleeding! No, no, no. I can't lose him. I won't!

Fear and fury galvanized me into action. That little jerk was not going to take Will away from me. No way. Ears ringing from the gunshot, I ran around the glass case and picked up the weapon, hefting it in both hands. "Get up, Brian." The calm in my voice amazed me as did the steadiness of my fingers as I aimed the pistol. "Now."

"Just take it easy, little lady." He released Will and stood slowly, his hands raised, eyeing me with trepidation. "That thing could go off again if you're not careful."

"Will?" Stomach churning, I moved along the length of the counter, and kept the gun focused on Brian. Adrenalin raced through my veins, giving me an unfamiliar yet heady sense of power. "Are you okay?"

"The bastard shot me." Will's voice was filled with incredulity. "He shot me."

"I didn't shoot you." Brian scowled. "You hit my arm and made the gun go off."

By this time, Sarah had managed to get to her feet and was steadying herself on the jewelry display. "Grab a couple of those fancy designer scarves, Julie, and let's tie this son of a bitch up."

I gave her the gun, grateful to hand the damn thing over, and pulled two strips of colorful fabric from the scarf rack.

"Now, look, ladies. There's no reason to get all bent out of shape here. We've just had a little misunderstanding, that's all."

Brian blinked and his lower lip trembled. "Let's talk. We can straighten this out."

"Oh, *now* he wants to talk." Sarah scoffed and shook the gun in his direction. "Don't mess with me, you little jerk, or I'll go all Dirty Harry on your ass." She pointed to a wicker armchair in the center of the store. "Get your butt over there and sit down. Take off your clothes first, I don't want blood all over my white chair."

"I only wanna find Jeannie." Tears spilled over his cheeks as he backed his way to the chair, stripping off his jacket and shirt and dropping them on the floor. "I didn't want any trouble. I love her." He plopped down in the chair. "I miss her."

"Are you really *this* stupid, Jenner?" Sarah gave his own words back to him. "I'm not buying the tears again, sparky. Shut up or I'll let Julie here stuff a scarf in your mouth."

Now my hands shook with fear and impatience. I only wanted to get him secured so I could tend to Will.

"His hands behind him first, Julie," Sarah ordered. "Then tie his ankles to the chair."

Just as I tied the last knot around Brian's ankles and the chair leg, sirens screamed in the street outside. Resisting the urge to kick the bastard in the balls, I ran to Will as police officers swarmed the shop.

CHAPTER 24

"I'm going in there."

"Ms. Miles, wait—" A frustrated nurse called out as I cruised the cubicles in the emergency room, looking for Will.

"Sorry, but there's no way you're gonna keep me out of there another second." I peered around a curtain. No sign of Will.

The nurse gave a frustrated sigh. "Okay. He's in Number 8." She ran ahead of me, her white Crocs squeaking on the polished linoleum. "Come with me."

When she drew back the curtain, I slipped around her. Will lay in the bed, eyes closed, five o'clock shadow showing clearly against the pallor of his skin. An almost-empty IV bag dripped clear liquid into the crook of his arm, and his shoulder was wrapped in a white bandage.

The nurse rolled her eyes at me. "This one's been a very large pain in the behind tonight." She jerked a thumb in his direction as she moved to the other side of his bed to check the machines surrounding him. "We practically had to sedate him to get him to lie still while the doc patched him up. Pain meds finally kicked in."

"Did they get the bullet out?" I whispered, not wanting to disturb his rest. He looked so peaceful.

"Wasn't there. It was a clean entry and exit, so no surgery required. He'll be sore for a little while, but he'll heal." She pulled the blanket up under his arms before heading out the door. "This is getting low. I'll be right back."

I edged closer to the bed. He was so pale and still, if it weren't for the slight rise and fall of his chest, I'd have thought he was dead. When I reached out to touch his unbandaged shoulder, he opened his eyes.

"Hey, Slugger." He started to lift his head, but then dropped it back on the pillows. "My head hurts."

"I know. Lie still." I stroked his hair back from his forehead. "You hit your head when you and Brian fell."

He tried but failed to smile. "I think I've got a fat lip, too." The words slurred and he licked his dry lips.

"Yup, you do." I poured some water from the bedside pitcher and helped him manage the straw. "I still can't believe you rushed that idiot."

"Pretty stupid, huh?" He shrugged with a chuckle that immediately turned into a grimace. Apparently, even that small movement sent pain searing through him.

The nurse, who'd just returned with a new IV bag, ruffled his blond hair and shook her head. "Just found out we're keeping you overnight, buddy." Then she smiled at me. "They'll be moving him up to a room shortly."

Will turned more ashen and closed his eyes for a second. I could tell he hurt too much to argue, which was just as well since I had already planned on begging them to keep him anyway, and hadn't intended to take any crap from him about it. I wanted to be completely sure he was going to be okay before I took him home.

I met the nurse's gaze over his head, but she only shook her head. "He's going to be fine. They just want to watch the bump on his head. He's not concussed, but we keep head wounds for twenty-four hours." She switched out the IV and then scurried out, yanking the curtain halfway closed.

Tears pricked my eyes and I scooted a chair closer to the bed. I needed to touch him. I slid my left hand under the blanket and placed it on his belly. It was contact, and he didn't object.

In fact, he rubbed his fingers over mine, pressing my hand to his stomach, almost as if he needed me as much as I did him. "Thank God, they took that loon away." His voice was rough.

"Oh yeah, he's in custody. I'm sure he'll be locked up for a long time. Will, what were you doing at the shop? Carrie told me you were in Budapest." He looked so exhausted, I backpedaled and started to pull my hand away. "Never mind. You rest. We'll talk later."

He heaved a big sigh and stroked his fingers from my elbow to my wrist. "No, I want you here. Stay, please."

His words warmed me to my toes so I settled back into the chair. "Do you feel like telling me how you got from Eastern Europe to the shelter?"

Curling his fingers around mine under the blanket, he met my gaze, emotion filling his azure eyes. "It was kinda weird. I got into O'Hare this afternoon and caught a cab to head home, but for some reason, I suddenly had this overwhelming feeling that I needed to see *you*. It was like I was—was being pushed. I just *had* to get to you immediately. I knew it was your day at the shop, so I told the cabbie to take me to there."

"I've never been so happy to see someone in my entire life." I didn't mention the prayer I'd breathed to the heavens—to Charlie—just before Will had appeared at the door. I'm not a particularly spiritual person, but I was convinced Charlie had sent Will to me. "Will, I—"

"And here's the dynamic duo." A voice from the doorway interrupted me, and there was Sarah in a wheelchair, her red head bandaged. Dismissing the orderly with a smile and a thank you, she wheeled herself closer to the bed. "You two are quite a pair. How ya doin', hero?" With a crooked grin, she started to rise, then plopped back into the chair, her face contorted in pain.

"Sarah, what the hell are you doing up?" I hopped up to straighten the pillow behind her back and rearrange the blanket over her knees. When I'd left her earlier, she'd been resting comfortably in a cubicle a few yards away from Will.

"I was bored all by myself, so I thought I'd come over and check on our boy. You only look a little worse for the wear, Lancelot." She gave Will a thumbs up. Concern showed in her green eyes in spite of her casual manner.

"I'm okay. Sore shoulder and a raging headache." His mouth twisted. "You must have one too. God, Sarah, that guy totally coldcocked you."

"Aw hell, I've had worse than this from old butthead. But they're saying I have to stay overnight for observation anyway." She turned to me. "How're you doing, Jules?"

"I'm fine." I went over to the bed again and reached for Will's hand. "*I'm* not the one who got pistol whipped or shot."

Sarah squirmed to get comfortable in the wheelchair. "I could *not* believe that little jerk came back. And hey, for the record, I have no idea where Jeannie flew to, but it sure as hell wasn't back to *our* shelter. She knows they'd have turned her away for giving any information to her horse's ass of a husband." She rolled her eyes in a show of obvious disgust. "I couldn't believe our hero here"—a head nod to Will—"charging that guy like a roaring lion."

"A roaring lion? Seriously?" Will sputtered, dull red color filling his cheeks. "I have no memory of *roaring*, only of being focused on stopping him from taking Julie away."

"You roared, Will. Loud enough to wake the dead," Sarah drawled. "

"Oh, Will, for God's sake—" I gaped at him, suddenly horrified all over again at what could've have been. "You could've been killed. What on earth possessed you?"

He dropped his eyes. "You two are giving me way more credit than I deserve. All I could think of was making sure the bastard didn't take you away. He was scared and stupid. Either of you probably could've taken him."

"But he had a gun!"

He shrugged, then winced.

"Will—" Tears finally overflowed onto my cheeks as I gazed at him, overwhelmed at the fact that he'd risked his life for me.

Trembling like an adolescent on a first date, he tugged me closer. "Can I confess something?"

I nodded, heedless of the tears streaming down my face.

He took a deep breath. "Once, a long time ago, in Willow Bay, I passed you and Charlie down on the beach. You were staring at him like—like he was some kind of superhero, and I remember thinking, *Wow, how would it feel to have someone look at me that way?*"

I opened my mouth to speak, but he stopped me with a finger against my lips and a brief shake of his head.

"From the first day I saw you in Carrie and Liam's apartment, I've wanted to see *that* same expression in your eyes when you looked at me. The way you're looking at me right now." He let his finger slip ever so slowly over to brush my cheek, wiping away the tears. "If I'd known it was going to take both of us damn near getting killed for me to see it, I'd have arranged for us to run into a mugger a couple of months ago."

Out of the corner of my eye, I saw Sarah wheel herself backward toward the door. She gave me a wink and a wave as the curtain dropped behind her.

I placed one hand on his cheek. "You saved my life," I

murmured. "But you don't have to be a superhero. I don't want a superhero. Just be you, okay?"

"Well, I'm not really the hero type, but I couldn't let him hurt you." He smiled at me modestly. "I've got plans for us, darlin'."

Our eyes met and locked. Leaning down, I pressed my lips to his in a soft kiss. "I love you, Will."

W ill and I holed up in his apartment together for a week after he was released from the hospital. I was an excellent nurse, providing chicken soup, hot tea, and sympathy, while he groused about being an invalid. Charlie would've basked in the extra attention and had me running hither and yon. Will worried I was doing too much for him.

"Jules, I'm good here. Come sit down." He patted the sofa next to him one late afternoon after I'd helped him shower and dress before trying to decide what to cook for supper. He'd opened a bottle of wine and it sat on the coffee table with two glasses. "Chill, babe. Here, have a glass of wine."

I smiled gratefully and plopped down, resting my head on his good shoulder before pouring for both of us.

"To us." Will touched his glass to mine. "*I'm* cooking tonight. What do you want?"

"Whatever you want is fine."

He tossed me a frown. "Sorry, you cooked that last night. Give me a choice, please."

This had become our song and dance whenever a decision needed to be made. Will insisted I give him a preference. He didn't always agree, and we didn't constantly go with my choices, but he asked.

To my great surprise, he even let me see his own imperfections, never once trying to hide who he really was in order to impress me. Will Brody had nothing to prove to me or anyone else. His proclivity for messiness showed up immediately and made me very grateful he had someone come in to clean once a week. The man simply didn't get why a bed had to be made every day or why dust on the TV screen bugged me.

We found compromises, rather than me simply giving in to his every whim and foible. The occasional late-night cigars were banished to the balcony, and somehow his towel began being hung neatly on the rack instead of slung over the top of the shower after he'd found me cleaning up the bathroom one morning.

In turn, I stopped believing it was my job to keep the pantry and fridge stocked with his favorite trail mix or the sparkling water he preferred. After duplicating his purchases more than once, I discovered it could be fun to wander the aisles of the market *together*—something that would never have occurred to Charlie. Never once did I get up in the wee hours to redo my makeup, and on laundry day, I left his underwear and socks in heap on the bed for him to fold and put away. Small things, but significant.

Will clearly adored the confused, silly, menopausal, some-times-difficult Julie—the one who was learning to ask for what she wanted, even demand her own way if it suited her. His patience and kindness never once faltered, not when I griped about not having enough help at the shop, changed my mind five times about what I wanted to eat, or whined about nothing at all.

He wasn't interested in the Julianne Miles that I'd invented for Charlie, not the perfect little housewife who'd remained at her husband's beck and call. Every word, every action demonstrated his expectation that we be *partners* as well as lovers. That made him all the more dear.

I loved him for his unassuming ways, for caring what I thought, for listening to me, and considering what I had to say.

And I tested him despite myself. I threw hissy fits. I pouted. I gave him a million irrational reasons to give up on me as I worked through the last vestiges of pain left from Charlie's betrayal.

But he was having none of my nonsense. He stood fast, teasing me, holding me, showing me in his own special, quiet way how much he loved me. I knew whatever else my future held, this man was my destiny.

That night, we made love for the first time since he'd been released from the hospital and laughed 'til our sides ached, trying to come up with a position that didn't hurt his shoulder or pop his stitches. Laughter turned into kisses that ignited the incredible chemistry between us, his touches once again making me mindless, taking me outside myself.

The bedroom was another place where Will Brody had nothing to prove. I was there. I was present and never once worried about whether or not I pleased him. I *knew* I pleased him —it showed in every caress, in each kiss, in the love that smoldered in his eyes as we moved together.

Afterward, he cuddled me close, not one bit worried about my tousled hair or lack of makeup. Long into the night, we planned our summer together, talking about the fun we'd have in Michigan, deciding whether I should meet him in Budapest or Paris or Athens as he went on tour with Liam.

We weren't perfect, but we didn't have to be. No one had ever loved me with such purity of heart or total acceptance, and I loved him completely, or at least I thought I did. In spite of all of it, a trace of doubt remained. Was it a little leftover fear that I could once again be wrong about the man I loved? Or perhaps some lingering question about my love for Charlie?

CHAPTER 25

"Everything was absolutely perfect, Jules." Carrie swept out her arms as if to embrace the entire ballroom at the Stamford. The evening was winding down and we'd taken a break from the dancing. "I swear I don't know how you pulled this off in only two and half months, particularly since you spent part of that time taking care of Will."

"She certainly did." Will wiggled his brows and flicked an imaginary cigar, Groucho-style while Carrie giggled and I blushed.

"You can clean this guy up and put him in tux, but he's still just that lewd California beach bum, looking for attention," Liam observed as he stopped a server making a final round with glasses of Champagne.

"*I'm* talking about my recuperation, Maestro. I don't know where your dirty-old-man mind was headed." Will raised both hands with an angelic smile before grabbing a flute of sparkling wine and taking a sip.

"I love how these two pretend to be so suave and debonair just 'cause they're all dressed up, don't you, Caro?" We linked arms and I touched my glass to hers in a private toast. "We've seen them in their baggy shorts and faded t-shirts down on the beach, being total nerds with the metal detectors."

"That's right, they can't fool us."

"It's hard *not* to feel suave and debonair when you're with the two most gorgeous women in the room." Will winked, but the look he gave me told me he meant every word. "Those vintage outfits are unbelievable. Did they really wear backless dresses in the 1930s?"

"This *is* an original." I twirled around slowly, glancing back over my shoulder with what I hoped was a sultry smile as his eyes drank me in like a man dying of thirst.

The cream, silk crepe Worth gown that our vintage clothing expert from the auction house had dated to circa 1935 fit me like it had been tailor-made. The fabric moved sensuously against my bare skin—of course, it being backless, wearing a bra was out of the question. Once I tried it on, I couldn't resist modeling it, although it'd been years since I'd been on a catwalk. I was nervous, but the crowd had *ooh*ed and *aah*ed when I stepped out on the runway, and the appreciation in Will's eyes told me it was the right decision.

For fun, Carrie took a walk, too, sensational in a yellow silk beaded chemise with a gold embroidered bolero jacket from the 1920s—another of the treasures we'd found in the donated clothing. We'd also convinced Sarah to take to the runway in the Fortuny jacket she'd fallen in love with that terrible day back in March. I'd secretly asked Liam to bid on it for me, so soon it would belong to her. It would be the perfect farewell gift when I went back to Michigan for the summer.

Miraculously, Jeannie's ox of a husband hadn't managed to get to the table where Sarah and I had laid out the precious antique clothing. Not a single outfit was harmed, and the nine vintage pieces had sold for amazing sums. Even the auctioneer had been stunned at the prices they'd brought. We discovered that the antique clothing had been donated by one of Carrie's older symphony patrons, who had no idea the items she was giving away were so valuable. Sarah and I agreed that we had to tell her, but when we contacted her, she simply brushed our concerns aside, telling us how happy she was to help out our cause.

Those items and the other couture gowns and designer pieces that had been donated, along with ticket sales, were going to provide enough income to keep La Belle Femme and the shelter in business for at least a couple more years. All in all, our fundraiser was turning out to be a huge success.

Naomi and Carl Fox's vast resources and unflagging energy had set the show in motion even as I tended to a recuperating Will and ran the shop for Sarah. With great delight, she turned my former employers loose to create an incredible benefit fashion show, dinner, dance, and auction. I'm still not sure how they managed it, but by the time I was able to leave Will and jump in with both feet, they'd already chosen a menu with the caterer, picked the music for the evening, and arranged the entire fashion show.

All that was left was for me was to work with the auctioneer and his staff of experts, inventorying the items for sale. Bidding was silent and high-tech, with each guest being given a type of smart phone with a program listing all the clothing. On it, they could cruise the items from the fashion show and make their bids. Volunteers, most of them women from the shelter, sat at tables behind the scenes, accepting bids electronically at laptops on loan for the event from the auction house. I'd slipped back to check on our total, and the sum overwhelmed me.

We had Carrie to thank for the incredible turnout—she'd come to the Windy City to promote the event among Chicago patrons of the arts, businesses, and her friends. We sold out of tickets days before the benefit and had people clamoring for more. The ballroom filled to capacity, a sight that thrilled all of us associated with the shelter. Apparently, Chicago had figured out it was important to stop domestic violence—some guests had already asked if this was going to be an annual event. That idea intrigued me enough, I'd started making mental notes for another benefit. I knew I'd be here. My heart was not only firmly tied to La Belle Femme, but also to Chicago.

And most of all to Will.

"Jules? Dance with me?" Will's hand on my shoulder brought me back to the ballroom as the orchestra began playing Hoagy Carmichael's "The Nearness of You."

He held his arms out, and I slipped into them. We eased onto the crowded dance floor, his hand warm on the bare skin on my lower back. He sang the lyrics to the old song softly in my ear as we danced. Eyes closed, I curled my fingers into the hair that grew over his collar and allowed him to tug me closer. We moved together among the other dancers, wrapped up in our own little world.

I opened my eyes for a moment, hoping to catch Carrie's attention for a quick sisterly thumbs-up when she and Liam passed by us. Instead, what I saw took my breath away.

Charlie Miles lounged against the doorway of the ballroom, elegant in a white dinner jacket and perfectly pressed black pants. Dear God, there was my husband dressed to kill—his grey hair swept back from his handsome face, arms crossed over his chest, and a small knowing smile playing on his full lips. My eyes widened. I raised my head from Will's shoulder and gasped a quick breath as Charlie winked and gave me a small nod. Shutting my eyes in disbelief, I tried to catch my breath, but when I opened them again, he'd disappeared.

"You okay?" Will pulled back to stare down into my face.

"I–I thought I saw… "I gazed all around us, searching the crowd, even though I knew there was no way I'd find him. Whoever I'd seen couldn't possibly have been Charlie. For a few seconds I stood still in Will's arms on the dance floor, waiting for the wave of resentment that always materialized when I thought of Charlie. But it never came. All that was inside me was joy, pure wondrous joy. I'd been released. It was my final moment of liberation. In a weird way, Charlie had come through again, just like he had when he'd sent Will to me at the shop. Now, I was certain his appearance there had been Charlie's doing, answering my plea for help. And here he was again, letting me know it was time to move on and be happy—with Will.

"Jules?" Will's handsome face came into focus. "Honey?"

"I'm sorry. I was suddenly sort of… overwhelmed."

"With what? How devastatingly handsome I am in a tux? Or my awesome dance moves?"

That wicked grin sent a spasm of delight straight through me. Right there in the middle of the dance floor, I threw my arms around his neck, kissing him with all the love and passion I had in me.

"I love you, Will Brody," I whispered. "I want to spend the rest of my life showing you exactly how much."

His expression filled with a love so intense I couldn't bear to look away from him. "Now those are the words I've been waiting to hear," his voice cracked slightly.

"Want to get out of here? Go home where I can *show* you just how much I love you?" I wiggled my brows, trying for his earlier Groucho imitation.

"You bet, Slugger." He kissed me hard before wrapping his arms around me and waltzing me back into the crowd that still swayed to the music. "Just as soon as we finish this dance."

Once More From the Top

What do you do when the one who got away…comes back?

Carrie Halligan never regretted the choice she made sixteen years ago to raise her son Jack by herself in Willow Bay, Michigan. A successful photographer by day, at night Carrie satisfies her musical passions by playing piano at a hotel bar, maintaining a balance that works for her and Jack. Walking away from Maestro Liam Reilly without telling him she was pregnant with his child may have been the hardest thing she'd ever done, but it was definitely the right thing.

When Liam shows up in town to perform a benefit concert with the local symphony, however, Carrie's carefully crafted life spins out of control. After sending Jack to summer camp, she realizes she can't keep Liam in the dark forever. Telling the truth to the man she once loved more than life itself isn't near as hard as spending time in his presence and realizing that the years haven't diminished his power over her heart. Will her lie be too much to get past, or will the spark of passion between them overcome everything?

Available at: Amazon | Barnes and Noble | Kobo | Smashwords

The Summer of Second Chances

It's never too late to start over…

When Sophie Russo inherits two lakeside cottages in Willow Bay, Michigan, she thinks she can start over with a peaceful, quiet summer.

Boy, is she wrong.

First, there's Henry Dugan, the nerdy genius behind the GeekSpeak publishing empire, who has rented Sophie's second cottage so he can write his novel. The instant attraction catches them both off guard. He's fresh off a brutal divorce, and Sophie's still grieving her beloved Papa

Leo, so this is no time to start a relationship, but a casual summer fling might be an option…

Then Sophie's long-lost mother barrels onto the scene and opens up a long-buried mystery involving Depression-era mobsters and a missing cache of gold coins worth millions that some present-day hoodlums would like to get their hands on.

Suddenly, Sophie's quiet summer becomes a dangerous dance with her grandfather's dark past. With Henry at her side–and in her bed–Sophie needs to find a way to make peace with the past and look toward the future… assuming she lives that long.

Available at Amazon.com | Barnes and Noble.com | Kobo| Smashwords

Saving Sarah

She thought she'd never feel safe again. She was wrong.

When Sarah Bennett's abusive ex hunts her down in Chicago, her friends spirit her away to Willow Bay, where she hopes to begin again with a different identity. But terror keeps her holed up, unable to start her new life.

Deputy sheriff Tony Reynard never expected to be staring down the barrel of a gun when he enters Sarah's apartment to finish up some handyman work, but that's how the fiery little redhead greets him, and he's beyond intrigued.

After an intervention by her loving friends, Sarah becomes involved in a project to turn an old mansion into a battered women's shelter. The women work together to renovate the house, along with the help of the townspeople and the delectably handsome Tony, who is a true renaissance man. Tony vows to bring Sarah back to life and love, but knows he needs to move slowly to win her heart.

When her ex tracks her down once more, Sarah must find the courage to protect her friends and her new love from his wrath.

Available at Amazon.com | Barnes and Noble.com | Kobo | Smashwords

ABOUT THE AUTHOR

Nan Reinhardt is a *USA Today* bestselling author of romantic fiction for women in their prime. Yeah, women still fall in love and have sex, even after 45! Imagine! She is also a wife, a mom, a mother-in-law, and a grandmother. She's been an antiques dealer, a bank teller, a stay-at-home mom, a secretary, and for the last 20 years, she's earned her living as a freelance copyeditor and proofreader.

But writing is Nan's first and most enduring passion. She can't remember a time in her life when she wasn't writing—she wrote her first romance novel at the age of ten, a love story between the most sophisticated person she knew at the time, her older sister (who was in high school and had a driver's license!) and a member of Herman's Hermits. If you remember who they are, *you* are Nan's audience! She's still writing romance, but now from the viewpoint of a wiser, slightly rumpled, menopausal woman who believes that love never ages, women only grow more interesting, and everybody needs a little sexy romance.

Visit Nan's website: www.nanreinhardt.com
Facebook: https://www.facebook.com/authornanreinhardt
Twitter: @NanReinhardt
Talk to Nan at: nan@nanreinhardt.com

Made in United States
North Haven, CT
09 February 2022